That Holiday in France

By Rhoda Baxter

Get a free novella when you sign up to my newsletter.

Details are at the end of this book.

Enjoy *That Holiday in France*. ☺

That Holiday in France
Rhoda Baxter

Chapter 1

A*pril* Ellie was late getting home because of the rain. She shook her umbrella out on the doorstep, and rushed in to put it in the kitchen sink before it dripped everywhere.

"That you, our Ellie?" her dad said, from the living room.

"Yes, it's me." She took off her coat and hung it up.

"What've you got for us today?"

She popped her head round the door to find her dad sitting in his chair, still in his work overalls but without his shoes, with the telly on low. "How was work?" she asked him.

He shrugged. "Same as ever. How about you? How's the cakes?"

"Not bad," she said. "I've got some apricot tarts and a few bits of fruit cake."

His eyes crinkled into a hint of a smile. "Ah. Lovely."

"Do you want another cuppa to go with it?"

He nodded, drained his mug and held it out to her.

Ellie went into the living room to take it from him. Close up, he looked tired and, to Ellie's surprise, old.

Back in the kitchen she frowned as she made the tea. Strong tea, two sugars for Dad. Milky tea, one sugar for her. She popped two of the apricot tarts and the crumbling cake on a plate. The best perk from working in the bakery was that she got to take home some of the cakes that were too wonky or broken to sell. She saved the least damaged apricot tart to give to Luke.

She looked at the clock. Oh no. Later than she'd thought.

She rushed through, two mugs clutched in one hand, the plate with the cakes in the other. She pushed the door open with her bum and backed in.

"Here you go, dad." She put his mug down on the side table next to him, nudging the remote control out of the way.

"Ah, you're a good gel," he said. He picked up a tart and examined it. It had an apricot half embedded in frangipane. The cakes in the shop had a delicate glaze over the top. Being a reject, this particular tart had singed a little on the top. "This looks fancy."

"It's Sue's new recipe," she said. "I've not tried it yet." She grabbed her own and said, "I can't stay down here and chat, dad. Luke's coming over in a bit to pick me up. I'd better get ready."

He looked disappointed, but nodded. "There's some post for you. Nice, posh looking envelope." He nodded towards the windowsill, where the post usually ended up. The days were lengthening, so the curtains were still open. When her mother had been around, the curtains were drawn and the lights were on by now.

Ellie stifled a sigh and put her tart back on the plate. She turned on the lights, rescued the post and drew the curtains. The net curtain was looking a little grey. She'd have to wash them again soon, once it stopped raining quite so much. She looked down at the post. The envelope was creamy and thick. "That is fancy," she said, quietly.

"You going to open it, then?"

She sank down onto the small two seater sofa and opened it, trying not to tear too much. The postmark was foreign. For one insane second, she thought maybe Mum was writing to her.

"Oh, hurry up, lass," her father said. He was clutching his mug of tea and leaning forward.

She winced as the lovely paper tore at the end and pulled out a card. A wedding invitation. She opened it and quickly scanned what was inside. "Oh my god!" She giggled and put her hand over her mouth. "You'll never guess what, dad. You remember Sophie from school? She's getting married."

"Oh aye." He leaned back again, and brought his tea up to his face to blow on it. "What's she doing now? Went somewhere down south didn't she?"

"She went to university," Ellie said. She herself had stopped going to school at seventeen and taken on more hours at Sue's bakery. She didn't regret it, mind, but sometimes she wondered what it must be like to leave Trewton Royd and go somewhere else. Most of her friends who had left had drifted away, out of her orbit, but Sophie had stayed in touch. "She got a job in France last summer and stayed there."

"Who's she marrying then?" her father said. "Anyone we know?"

"Ethan. She met him at university." Ethan was tall and handsome and French. Hence Sophie's move to France.

There was a note written on the inside of the invitation. 'Ellie, I know it's a long way, but I hope you can come. There will be a few people from Trewton there, but not many. Ethan's grandparents have this fabulous old place. If you RSVP before the end of next month, I can try and save a room for you and

Luke. If not, there's also lots of space to pitch a tent in the garden. I really hope you can be there. Love Sophie'.

"Aww," she said. "She's getting married in France. How exciting."

Her father sniffed. "Shame you won't be able to go," he said. "Bit rude that, sending you an invite knowing you can't come. Rubbing your face in it."

"What?" She looked up. "Who says I'm not going?"

"Well y'aren't are ye?" he said. "It's bloody expensive and it's all the way in that Europe. We're trying to get out from under bloody Europe. We don't need to be travelling across to France, swelling their coffers." He turned his face back to the telly. "Bloody Europe. Bloody Europeans."

Ellie sighed. This again. "It's been ten years," she said. "And I'm not Mum."

No response. "I'll have Luke with me, anyway."

"Didn't stop your mum, did it?" It was a growl.

Ellie opened her mouth to argue and then shut it. What was there to say? They had gone on holiday and while Dad slept off his hangover, Mum had met Arno and fallen in love. It had taken another two years of furtive calls and meetings before she left, but Dad had never trusted anything European since. Or women. She put the card carefully back into the envelope. "I'll talk to Luke and see what he thinks."

"You do that," said her father. "He'll tell you the same as me. You'll see."

Ellie tucked the envelope into her waistband, grabbed her tea and the plate which now only had one pastry on it and made for the door. "If you need me," she said. "I'll be upstairs getting ready."

LUKE, WHEN HE ARRIVED, wasn't impressed with the invitation. "Oh, she's getting married in France, is she? What's wrong with Yorkshire? Not good enough for her?"

"I dunno, I think it sounds nice, having a wedding in France." Ellie had never been to France. Dad had refused to let her go on the school's French exchange trip. She thought of the family she'd seen on *Location, Location, Location*, who had all moved to a French chateau. "I think it sounds dead romantic." She put the envelope carefully back on her bedside table.

Luke rolled his eyes. "I didn't know you were even in touch with Sophie."

"She's my best friend!"

"Was, love. Was. She's barely looked at any of us since she went off to uni." Luke stood and looked at his watch. Clearly, it was time to go.

"We go out for a drink every time she comes home." She realised how defensive she sounded. Sophie didn't come home often, it was true. But she did email a couple of times a week at least, and when they met up, it took a few minutes for them to catch up, and the months fell away. "We talk to each other a lot, thanks."

"Course you do." Luke gave Ellie an affectionate pat on the bottom before clattering down the stairs. He popped his head into the living room. "We'll be off now, Roy," he said to Ellie's dad.

"Have a good time," Dad said.

When Ellie joined Luke, her father said, "See you later, then, love."

They set off in the balmy evening to walk to the pub. It was quiz night. Ellie put her hands in the pockets of her denim jacket. Luke gently teased one of her hands out and curled his big, warm hand around it.

"I know it'd be nice to go to Sophie's do," he said. "But face it, babe, we can't afford to go to France, even if we wanted to. We're saving up, remember. For when we move in together."

"Yes, I know, but maybe we could -"

"You want to spend money that we're saving so that we can start our own future, to go to someone else's wedding?" said Luke. "Don't be daft." He tucked her hand into his arm and strode on.

Ellie hurried along, to keep up. Their future. Everyone talked about it as though it was a done deal. She and Luke had been together for nearly four years, since she was seventeen, and they were going to get married. Fact. Except Luke hadn't actually asked her to marry him ... or even to move in with him.

"Luke," she said, as they got to the end of the main road that wound its way down towards the village. "You know you haven't asked me yet."

"Asked you what?"

"To move in with you. You've just assumed we would."

He stopped walking and turned to face her. "We talked about it. I don't have to propose. It's not like getting married."

"I don't think we did discuss it," said Ellie. "You just said."

"Ellie," said Luke. "What are you trying to say? Do you not want to move in with me? Is that what this is about?"

She looked at him, at his eyes which were narrowed in annoyance, at his scowl. He wasn't very nice when he looked like that. He was much bigger than she was. When they'd first got together, she had loved the way he stood protectively by her. Now, just sometimes, she wasn't so sure what he was protecting her from.

"Well?" he said. "Because if that's what you're saying, we may as well not bother with any of this." He shook her hand out from the crook of his arm and stepped closer. "What are we doing going out together if we don't move in together? Where's the future in that?" He was very close. She fought the urge to step back.

She shook her head. "That's not what I meant," she said. "Forget I said anything, it's all fine."

"Is all this fuss because I said you can't go to that wedding in France?"

"No, it's fine. Let's go. We need to get to the pub before the quiz starts." She started off again, he paused for a beat before following her.

THE PUB WAS BUSY, LIKE it always was on quiz night. The 'team', mostly men from the garage where Luke worked, were sitting in their favourite place - at a table by the quiz machine. Sometimes, one of the girlfriends came too, but not tonight. Luke went to get the drinks in, leaving Ellie to say hello to the guys. Someone had just finished a packet of peanuts. Ellie looked at it. "You know," she said. "I really fancy some peanuts." She got back to her feet. "Anyone else?" she asked.

"Get us another packet of ready salted, would you Ellie," one of the guys said.

When she got to the bar, Luke said, "Is something wrong?"

"No. Just fancied some peanuts." She smiled at Phil, the landlord. "Hiyya Phil. Can I have two packets of peanuts please - ready salted."

Phil passed her two packs and returned his attention to the pint he was pulling for Luke. Ellie passed some money to Luke, picked up the peanuts and turned to go.

"I've ordered us chips," Luke said.

"Lovely." They always had chips on quiz night. It served as a meal until they went back to hers, when she would make them late night cheese on toast before they went to bed. As she made her way back to the table, she wished Sophie were there. She liked Luke's friends, but there wasn't much that she could talk to them about. No one 'got' her like Sophie did.

Someone called her name. Ellie turned. A young man jumped up from his seat at a table not far away. He was thin, tall and brown skinned. "Hi Ellie."

She smiled. "Ash! Hiyya. How're you? How's uni?"

"Good. Good, thank you." He pushed his black hair back from his forehead.

"You're looking well," she said. He looked different since the last time she'd seen him. He seemed to have grown taller, and he was certainly more outgoing than he used to be. This time last year, he would barely have spoken more than a few words to her. Even that would have been at a mumble. "I almost didn't recognise you just now."

"Thanks, I think," he said, giving her a friendly smile. "I ... er ... did you hear from Sophie? About the wedding?"

"Oh yes, isn't it brilliant. A wedding in France sounds so exotic." She remembered that Sophie knew Ash quite well. They'd had some classes together. Physics or something.

He nodded, put his hands in his pockets and bounced a little on the balls of his feet. "Are you ... are you going?"

"Ah, no. Probably not."

"Oh?" He looked surprised. "Why not? Since you guys were friends, I thought ..."

Well yes. You would think she'd be going to her best friend's wedding. Ellie forced herself to smile. "Well, Luke-"

"Did someone mention my name?" Luke appeared beside her and put his arm around her. "Alright, Ass?"

Ellie winced.

Ash stilled at the old school nickname, and took his hands out of his pockets. "Luke."

"What are you two gossiping about?" said Luke, giving Ellie's shoulders a squeeze.

"Ash," Ellie said, pointedly, "was just asking if I was going to Sophie's wedding."

"Oh, she's not," said Luke.

Ash looked at Ellie, a question in his frown.

"Can't afford it," she said, quickly. "It's a shame, really. I'd have loved to go."

"You're going, I suppose," said Luke.

"I was thinking about it, yes." Ash's gaze moved from Luke, to the arm holding Ellie firmly and back to Luke. Suddenly, Ellie felt very small.

"I suppose you'll be dipping into your trust fund," Luke sneered.

Ash's eyes flicked upwards. "I don't have a trust fund."

"Yes, well it's okay for your sort," said Luke cryptically.

Ellie knew that Ash wasn't rich. He worked in the corner shop in the holidays. She had only spoken to him a few times, when she went to deliver the bread to the shop, and he seemed like a nice guy. She didn't know why Luke was being so weird. She gave Luke a quizzical look, which he ignored.

"Anyway, come on, love. Let's go sit down, shall we?" Luke steered her away.

She mouthed 'sorry' to Ash as she was led away. He raised a hand, as though to say it was fine.

"Did you have to be so rude?" she said to Luke.

"Well, he was hitting on my girl, so yes. He's lucky I didn't do worse."

"We were having a conversation. He was not hitting on me. He was asking me if I was going to my friend's wedding. Which I really should be."

Luke stopped and frowned. "What has got into you today, Ellie?"

For a second she was speechless. She fought to think of a response that wasn't just a wail of 'I want to go to Sophie's wedding'.

"Anyways," said Luke. "Looks like the quiz is starting."

And just like that, she missed her chance. Ellie sat down, threw one packet of peanuts across to the man who'd wanted them and tore open her own. Someone passed her the pen and paper with 'you've got the best handwriting'. She took it and bent her head so that no one could see her fume.

Chapter 2

June

Ellie grabbed her sandwich - prosciutto, tomato and basil with mayonnaise in thick slices of white bread. Being able to make her own sandwich from the menu was one of the perks of working at the bakery.

"Here," said Sue, the owner. "You can have this as well." She passed over one of her trademark cinnamon rolls, which had a split in one corner. "I dropped a pan on it."

"Thanks, Sue."

"Don't be late back, mind," said Sue, with a small smile.

"I've put an alarm on my phone," Ellie said. She stepped out of the shop into the sunshine. It was a beautiful day. Not hot, exactly, because of a chilly breeze, but still nice. She made her way to the church. There was a bench, a little way down, where she could sit with the stone church wall behind her and the view of the Pennines in front of her. As she crossed the road, she glanced at the corner shop where Ash worked in the holidays. He would be off to France for Sophie's wedding soon. She hated that she couldn't go.

Funny, she didn't often think about Ash, even though she'd seen him around at school and in the shop. In the summer, she would sometimes get to the bench to find him already there, eating his lunch, with a book in front of his nose. She never knew what he'd be reading. He said he picked up at least one book from the returned shelf and read that, because it was good to read widely. He was the only guy she knew who would admit to reading romances and Westerns alongside the Booker Prize shortlist. He had been painfully shy and hadn't really spoken much, but they often sat at opposite ends of the bench and ate in companionable silence.

Today, it was just her, so there was plenty of room for her to spread out. She ate her sandwich, pulled out her phone, and fired off a message to Sophie to check if she was free.

As she ate, she tried to imagine what it must be like to be Sophie, arranging a wedding in a far off country. When they were girls, growing up together, they had always vowed that they would stay together. They'd get married and live in houses next door to each other. Best friends forever. But life never did go according to plan, did it? It certainly didn't stick to plans made when you were in primary school. Sophie, always more into books than Ellie, had gone off to university and then to France. Ellie had stayed in Trewton Royd. But their friendship was strong enough that they'd kept in touch, despite the distance.

Ellie sighed, still chewing her lunch. It's a shame it wasn't strong enough for her to go to the wedding. Both Luke and dad acted like she was being hysterical about not being able to go. They probably had a point, but she missed Sophie terribly and the idea that she was having her big day without Ellie there … it hurt.

She finished her sandwich. A chilly breeze made her wish she was wearing a proper coat rather than her denim jacket. There was still a bit of time left before she had to be back at work, but there wasn't much point sitting here brooding, so she set off back to the bakery where she could sit in the warm and eat her slightly squashed cinnamon bun.

As she let herself in, her phone rang. She checked the display to see who it was.

"Sophie!" She tucked the phone between her chin and shoulder and shrugged her jacket off.

"Alright, bird," said Sophie. "Have you changed your mind yet?" She had been opening with this question ever since Ellie had told her she couldn't come to the wedding.

Ellie laughed. "No. I told you, I can't afford it. Anyway, how's it going?" She shifted the phone to her hand and took a seat. The cafe portion of the shop was empty. In the back, Sue was icing a birthday cake. She paused to see who had come in, then went back to her work.

"I can't believe you're not coming to my wedding," said Sophie. "Max has cried off too, so have James and Lucy. Which means the only person from school will be Ash. It's a pretty poor show when the only people from my side at the wedding are my parents, a couple of cousins and one friend!"

"I'm sorry, Soph." She hadn't really known the people Sophie was talking about. They'd all stayed to do A levels and go to university.

"Why doesn't Luke want to come? It'll be fun. Like a holiday. I mean, I know it's my wedding on one of the days, but for the rest, you could go sightseeing or whatever. My parents are doing a short holiday in Nice before they come to the wedding. You've always wanted to go to France, remember?"

"Did I?"

"You told me once that you won a French prize at primary school and you wanted to go and visit the places you read about in your textbook."

She frowned. She'd forgotten about that. Mum had been keen to take her to France the following year, but then the fateful holiday happened and all chances of her going abroad were well and truly squashed.

She sighed. "It sounds lovely, but Luke says we can't afford it." It really did sound lovely. One night, Ellie had looked up the area near the wedding venue. It looked amazing. Not far from the village where Sophie was getting married, was the Dordogne, which had amazing castles. She would have loved to go and see them. But Luke was right. It was expensive.

"How come Max isn't coming?" she said, to change the subject.

"Family crisis of some sort."

"Oh. Is his family all right?"

"Yeah. His mum's got to go in for a routine op and he needs to take care of his grandad."

"That's a shame." She didn't really know what to say to that. She didn't have a network of family, unlike most people in the village. Her dad was an outsider in that he'd grown up a few miles away. Mum had been the local. When Mum left, the village had somehow gathered around Ellie and her father. While Dad worked extra hours to make up for the loss of Mum's income, Ellie had been picked up by parents of friends until she was old enough to let herself into the house and fix her own tea. Between her dad's sister, who lived only twenty minutes away, Sophie's mum and the village, there was always someone keeping an eye out for her and Dad. Even the job at the bakery had happened because someone heard that Sue needed someone to help do the deliveries and pushed Ellie to go and ask about it.

"How about if I buy you a train ticket?" Sophie said, suddenly.

"What?"

"Max and Ash were meant to be travelling together. Ash has a spare ticket. If I got you a ticket, would you come to my wedding? It won't be the same without you there."

"But Luke -"

"Oh, stuff Luke. If he doesn't want to come, come without him! Please."

Ellie laughed. "I can't do that."

"He goes away without you. He went on that lads' trip to Tenerife when they finished school, remember?"

Ellie remembered. They hadn't been going out for very long at that time and she had missed him so much it hurt. Luke had been away with his friends a few times, but not recently. Not since they'd got serious. "I'm sorry, Soph," she said.

Sophie made a small 'mmm' sound. Ellie knew that sound.

"What are you plotting?" she said. "I know you're up to something."

"Nothing," said Sophie. "I've got a wedding to organise, love, I don't have time for other things." She cleared her throat. "Speaking of... I've got to run. Look, think about it. If you want to come without Luke, I'm sure I can sort something out. You'll have to sleep in a tent, but you'll be okay with that. It's not like we haven't been camping before."

Ellie smiled. When they were teenagers, she and Sophie often went camping together. That seemed so long ago now.

They chatted for a bit longer. When Ellie hung up, Sue came and leaned on the counter.

"Who was that? Sophie?" she said, casually wiping down the countertop, even though it didn't need it. "How are the wedding plans going?"

"She's really excited. It sounds amazing." Ellie carefully put her phone away.

"Is she having the big church wedding?"

"Registry office, I think. Ethan isn't hugely traditional and they've been living together for the last year anyway, so she says she doesn't want to get married in white. She's having a yellow dress, which she can wear again later if she wants to."

Sue nodded, approvingly. "I like that."

"I think Ethan's family are quite well off, not that you'd know to look at him," said Ellie. "They've got this house down in Bordeaux that his grandma lives in. She's letting them have the wedding there. From what Sophie said, she's going to have a big marquee in the grounds and caterers-"

"The grounds?" said Sue. "How big is this place?"

Ellie shrugged. "Sophie said it was old and crumbly." She leaned her elbows on the table. "Anyway, one of his aunts is doing the flowers. They're going for a super relaxed feel, apparently. I guess that makes sense seeing as half the guests are going to be camping in the garden. You can't really expect people to be formal with that."

"Who's doing the catering?"

"Local place," said Ellie. She clasped her hands and rested her chin on them. "I hate that I can't be there with her. I mean, if she was here, I'd be helping. I would have made her wedding cake if she let me."

Sue looked over her shoulder at the cake she had just finished. "I reckon you'd do a good job," she said.

"Really?" Ellie perked up. She helped Sue with some of the pastries and bakes for the shop, but she'd never thought of herself as a baker. Initially, she'd been hired just to do bread deliveries and to be a waitress, but over time, Sue had given her more to do. "You think I can bake? That means a lot, Sue."

Sue sniffed. "Well, you're not bad. With a bit of practice, I reckon you could bake like a good 'un." She smiled. "I think I've taught you well."

"Oh, thanks Sue. That's so kind of you."

Sue waved her thanks away. "So, why aren't you going to the wedding, then?"

"Luke."

The door pinged as someone came in. They both turned to see who it was. It was only Margie, Sue's best friend, who sometimes came in to sit in the cafe and do Sue's accounts.

Without needing to ask, Ellie got up, went behind the counter and started marking Margie's coffee.

Sue went back into the kitchen area and put the cake away. "What's Luke got against weddings?"

"Nothing. It's just that we can't afford it. And he thinks Ethan's poncey and I think ..." she dropped her voice. "I think he's worried I'll see Sophie's wedding and get fancy ideas about a wedding for us."

"What's this? What's this?" said Margie. "Are you getting married, Ellie?"

"No. No I'm not. Not yet."

Margie's face fell. "Oh. Okay. I love a good wedding." She looked meaningfully at her best friend.

Sue rolled her eyes. "Give over. Jack and I are not getting married. We're too old for that sort of nonsense."

"Never too old," said Margie, winking at Ellie. She went round the counter and disappeared into the office to get Sue's receipts.

Sue made herself a drink too and down with a sigh. "Oh, that's better." She stretched her legs out and rolled her shoulders. "You know," she said to Ellie. "It's not every day your best friend gets married. You should go. It'll be an adventure. And a holiday."

"That's what Sophie said," Ellie said, glumly. "But Luke says-"

"Oh, sod what Luke says. You should go anyway." Margie put the books on the table where Sue was and sat down next to her friend.

"I can't."

"Why not?"

"He'll be so cross."

Sue and Margie exchanged a glance. "Will he? Just because you want to go to your best friend's wedding?" said Sue, cautiously. "What else does he get cross about, love?"

Ellie frowned. Luke had strong views about things - about how the man was the head of the family, about what she wore, about where they went when they went out... but he wasn't a bad man. He was handsome, and strong and everyone liked him. He was hers. She was lucky to have him.

"I know what you're trying to do," she said to Sue. "You're trying to tell me he's being overpowering and all that. I've heard it before, okay, and he's not like that. He doesn't force me to do anything." She grabbed a pair of tongs and straightened out the biscuit display. "He tells me his opinions, but I don't have to agree with him. So he's not being a bully."

"But you do though, don't you, love," Margie said, gently. "You don't have to do as he says, but you always do. Because otherwise, he gets cross."

"No," said Ellie. "I don't do what he wants all the time. Mostly, we both want the same thing." She stalked into the kitchen and dealt with her plates.

When she came back out, Sue and Margie were both watching her. Ellie replenished the cinnamon buns and ignored them.

"You know, love," said Sue. "If it's about money, I can probably give you an advance of next month's wages, if you need it. I'd happily give you time off too. It would be a shame for you to miss your best friend's wedding. It's obvious that you want to go."

"It's fine." Ellie shook her head. "I won't know anyone and I don't speak French, so I won't know what's going on half the time." She finished what she was doing and took the empty bun basket back into the kitchen. "Anyway," she said, over her shoulder. "I don't want to talk about it."

Chapter 3

S ue and Margie didn't mention Luke again, but their conversation stayed in Ellie's mind. It nagged away at her while she made dinner for him, herself and dad. This was her regular Wednesday night. She made dinner for the three of them. Then Dad went out for his regular pub night with his friends, leaving her and Luke to spend some quality time together. Luke usually stayed over.

She added the tomato to the browned minced beef and thought over her own argument with Sue and Margie. She didn't let him get his own way. For example... she frowned. There had to be an example. Oh yes. He took her to see rom coms, which she knew he hated. There. See. There was an example. She smiled at the memory. She'd spent so long agonising over what to wear, that she was still in her school uniform when he'd knocked on the door. Wait. School uniform? She frowned again. That was four years ago. Had he really not taken her to see a rom com for four years?

Turning the hob down to let the chili simmer, she stepped back and drummed her fingers on the work surface. They must have been to the cinema since then. They'd been to see the Star Wars films and the Marvel ones, which she liked and he loved. Apart from that ... she slowly breathed out. The last fun thing she'd been to see was a Christmas rom com, with Sophie. Even that was a year ago.

Now that her brain had hit the groove, other things popped up into her mind. They used to do karaoke night and go clubbing and Luke had taken her to the Christmas markets in Leeds. None of that had happened in a long time. The last time they'd been anywhere that required her to dress up was when they went to the Christmas party at the local pub. She tidied up the kitchen, washing up all the pans and utensils so that there was less to do once Luke got here. He did the washing up and she dried and put things away. It was what she and her dad did on the nights that Luke wasn't here.

For a second, her future came into focus. It would be exactly like that. Night after night after night. She would move in with Luke and she'd swap around - so that she spent one or two evenings with Dad, making sure he had enough dinners to see him through the week and the rest of them with Luke. Nothing would change. This was her future. She'd somehow gone straight from school to middle aged with no stops in between. She was only twenty one!

The realisation was so strong, that she leaned against the work surface, breathless. All her life, she'd lived in Trewton Royd. She'd only ever been away for a weekend or, at most, a week in a caravan with Dad and her aunt Jane. Sophie had left to go to uni and met Ethan and was now having this glamorous wedding in France. Ash and the others, whom Sophie had befriended in the sixth form, when Ellie had started spending time with Luke ... they'd all gone off to uni now and would probably never come back. Even Luke had gone to training college before he returned to work for his father. Everyone was getting out leaving her behind.

Luke said he'd never wanted to leave. He didn't need anything much beyond the odd trip to Huddersfield, because everything he needed was right there in Trewton Royd. Ellie had always assumed that was all she wanted too. Now, she wondered if it was just that Luke had told her she wanted the same as him and she'd been too afraid to disagree.

Later, as they ate dinner, she watched Luke chatting away to her dad and wondered if she really was afraid of him, like Sue said. When she'd started going out with him, he had been the most gorgeous boy in school. He played football and was the guy that everyone wanted. Almost two years younger, Ellie had been giddy with excitement that he'd chosen her, out of all the girls in the school. He'd left school and started work full time at his Dad's garage. He would become manager of that place one day. He still played football on the weekend and he was still bloody gorgeous, and he was very much a man now.

In the beginning, Ellie had been too star struck to disagree with anything he said. He was older, cooler, of course he knew better. Somehow, that pattern had stuck. He still acted like he knew better. Did he? How did she know? She had never left this place. He had at least been away a few times. Perhaps he did know the world better than she did?

She ate another forkful of chili and rice. Her father liked Luke. Presumably, it helped that Luke's future was firmly in Trewton Royd. Ever since Mum left, Dad distrusted 'foreigners'. He considered Leeds to be the furthest you could go before people became foreign and untrustworthy. Since people had started talking about Brexit, he'd only become worse. Luke seemed to agree with him most of the time, so Ellie had taken it to be normal. But now, she wondered... Sophie, for example, never talked about politics with her. Was that because she thought Ellie wasn't interested? Or because they'd disagree?

"You're very quiet love, are you okay?" said Dad.

"Hmm? Yes. Sorry. I was just thinking about Sophie."

"When's the wedding? Next week?" said Luke. "Has she gone all bridezilla?"

"I can't imagine Sophie being that difficult," said Dad. "She always seemed like such a cheerful soul."

"She is," said Ellie. "She's been very cheery about it all. Her mum and dad are going out there this weekend. They're having a holiday before going to the wedding. She's a bit worried about the language barrier."

"Well, if she will marry a foreigner," said Dad.

"Ethan speaks really good English," said Ellie. "He's lovely. We've met him, haven't we Luke?"

Luke nodded. "Yes. Didn't have any trouble understanding him. He's a bit posh, but then, he's European and he's loaded."

Dad rolled his eyes. "Ah well, if Sophie's landed herself a rich bloke, then that's all to the good."

"That's a horrible thing to say," said Ellie.

There was a moment of silence, both men stopped eating to stare at her. She resisted the urge to apologise. "Sophie is not a gold digger."

"Never said she was, love," said her dad, in a soothing voice. "Just, that it's good that she's landed a rich bloke. If she's going to marry a foreigner, may as well be a rich one, eh?" he laughed, so did Luke. Ellie did not.

She didn't miss the glance that passed between the two men. She looked down and resumed eating. The conversation moved on to sport and whether or not the new road layout in the estate in the next village was going to cause traffic problems.

Afterwards, when Dad had gone out and she and Luke were washing up, Luke said, "What's got into you today, Ellie?"

She shook her head. She was still annoyed - at her dad and at Luke - but she couldn't work out exactly what was bothering her.

She carefully dried another plate and stacked it. The trouble was, she really, really wanted to go to Sophie's wedding and Luke hadn't even entertained the possibility. That hurt.

"Ellie?" Luke finished the last of the dishes and drained the sink. He took a corner of the tea towel she was holding and dried his hands. "It's not like you to snap at your dad like that. What's the matter?"

Ellie looked down at her hands. "I want to go to Sophie's wedding," she said, quietly.

"And I said, no," said Luke. "We can't afford it."

"If I can find the money-"

"I said no," said Luke firmly. That tone meant the subject was closed for discussion. This was what happened every time he didn't get his way. He got cross and shut the conversation down. And she let him. Sue was right. She was afraid.

"What about what I want?" said Ellie. "Does it not come into this? Sophie is my best friend. I should be there at her wedding. With or without you."

Luke froze. He stared at her for a minute in disbelief. "Well, you can't go without me, obviously. So you can't go."

Ellie looked at him. This time, she saw the handsome features twisted into a scowl. The big, normally gentle, hands half curled into fists. The tension in his jaw. This was the point where she normally backed down. He didn't like being contradicted, she knew that. So she never did it. Which meant that this relationship was run entirely on his terms.

She took a deep breath. "Luke, I really, really want to go. It's a chance for us to have a lovely, cheap holiday and go to my best friend's wedding at the same time. We never go on holiday, maybe this is our chance to do something different. We'll have to put our plans to move in together on hold for a few months, but it'd be worth it. Sophie is my best friend. Please." Her eyes filled with tears.

"No, Ellie. I said no, and that is final." He turned to walk out.

"But what about what I want?" Her voice was small and teary, but he heard.

"What?"

"We always do what you want. We never do what I want—"

"For fuck's sake, Ellie. You can choose what we watch tonight. Or where we go tomorrow. But we're not going to fucking France and that's final." He stomped off. "We're going to watch telly. Come on."

"No."

He paused, turned and took a deep breath. "Look. Babe," he said, in a voice that was straining to keep low. "I understand that you're feeling annoyed right now, but you have a think about it. You'll see that it's too expensive and, as much as you don't like it, I'm right."

"That's just it, isn't it? You always have to be right." Her voice shook. Something in the back of her mind screamed to back off, to keep things safe and predictable, but it seemed important that she didn't. The next time someone accused her of being too scared to stand up to Luke, she had to be able to say she wasn't.

Luke brought his hands up to his face and rubbed his palms over his temples, finger tensed. "Ellie. For fuck's sake. We can't afford it. You have to think long term. First it's 'let's waste money on a holiday', then it'll be 'let's rent a house we can't afford'. Where does it fucking stop? Eh?"

That did it. She may be naive and young, but she was never wasteful. She and her dad had managed on one salary until she was old enough to work. She had started her first job, doing the morning bread deliveries, at fourteen. She knew the value of money. Of all the things Luke could have accused her of. This was the wrong one to pick. "Now," she said. Tears spilled down her cheeks, but her voice was firm. "I think it ends now."

"What?" He stepped closer. He seemed bigger than before. "What are you talking about?"

"I think you should go, Luke." A step back and she felt the fridge at her back. She wrapped her arms around herself.

"Just because I won't let you—"

"No. Because you think you have the right to tell me I can't." She stepped back. "Please Luke. I want you to go."

He curled and uncurled his fists. "Ellie..." his voice was low and warning. He wasn't dangerous. He would never hurt her. She was sure.

She lifted her chin. "Please go, Luke." She blinked to clear the tears. "Go."

The fight seemed to drain out of him. He sighed. "Fine," he said. "We'll talk tomorrow. When you've come to your senses."

She stayed where she was while he grabbed his coat from the hallway. She listened as he walked out and slammed the door. She stayed there, arms wrapped around herself, shaking, for ten whole minutes, listening to the empty house. Slowly, she moved, locked the front door and went up to her room. She climbed into bed, fully clothed, pulled the duvet over her head and wept.

Chapter 4

The next day, Ellie felt awful, her eyes and throat hurt from all the crying she'd done the night before, but she felt oddly calm. Breaking up with Luke had seemed unthinkable a few days ago, but now, it was ... okay. Not pleasant, but manageable. It felt like it was the right thing to have done.

Sue and Margie had a point. When she thought about it, Sophie had been trying to tell her the same thing for ages. Luke wanted her to follow him like a puppy and when she didn't, he got angry and stormed out. It wasn't the basis for a good relationship, was it?

She got on with her work at the cafe. Sue kept trying to talk to her, but she'd managed to avoid anything more than the most superficial of conversations. Sue would find out eventually, but not yet. For today, Ellie needed to keep this raw secret to herself.

All her good intentions were thrown out of whack when Luke came to see her in his lunch break. He was still in his overalls when he came into the shop. Ellie was gathering up empty cups and plates. She froze, a tray held in front of her. Sue, who had been setting up a display of cupcakes, looked up.

"Hi Sue. Can I borrow Ellie for a couple of minutes?" Luke gave Sue a smile. He had a very charming smile.

Sue's gaze flicked to Ellie, asking her what she wanted to do. Ellie gave the smallest of nods.

"Five minutes," said Sue. "We're busy."

"Thanks." Luke turned to Ellie. "Can I talk to you for a minute, babe? Outside."

"Let me just put these in the back." She hurried round and put the tray by the sink. As she passed Sue, the older woman whispered, "I'm right here if you need me."

Ellie gave her a tiny smile. It was that knowledge that gave her the strength to go and talk to Luke in the first place. If she needed it, Sue would defend her. The fact that she felt she'd need defending, only reaffirmed that breaking up with Luke was the right thing to have done.

"Okay," she said to Luke, with a defiance she didn't really feel. "Let's go."

She followed him outside, her heart pounding. If he apologised now; if he could show her that he wasn't taking her for granted... then she would take him back. Maybe.

"Look," said Luke, without preamble. "About last night. Are you feeling better now?"

No apology, she noticed. She didn't reply.

"I get that I haven't paid you as much attention as usual these days. I've been so busy thinking about us moving in together and there's things going on at work, so ..." He gave a smile that normally melted her. "How about I take you out for dinner tomorrow? We can go to that Chinese place you like. Yeah? I'll come pick you up at seven."

Ellie drew herself up to her full height. "I notice you haven't apologised."

He frowned. "What for? It was just a stupid argument."

"For taking me for granted. For not listening to what I want." Her voice trembled and she hated that. She wished Sophie were here. Sophie always had her back.

"But babe, what you want is … "

"Is what? Stupid?"

"I was going to say 'not practical.'" He put his hands in the pockets of his overalls. "I mean, it's my money too, we should make joint decisions on how we spend it."

"Wait a minute," she said. "I'm not talking about your money. I'm talking about mine. There is no 'our money'. Not yet."

"Now hang on-"

"No. There is no 'our' anything, Luke. We're over. My stuff is my stuff. I'm not your wife. I'm not your property. I'm not even your girlfriend anymore."

His eyes narrowed. He took a step towards her. He wouldn't do anything to her here. Everyone could see. He wasn't actually dangerous. Ellie took a step back, her heart galloping. Suddenly, she wasn't so sure.

Behind her the door pinged. She looked over her shoulder. Sue had stepped out. Behind her was one of the regular customers.

Luke's gaze flicked to Sue. "Fine." His attention came back to Ellie. "Fine. Be like that. I don't need you." He turned to go, but then turned around again. "You'll be sorry. When your hormones or PMT or whatever the fuck this is calms down, don't come crawling back to me because I don't want an ungrateful bitch like you for a girlfriend."

Ellie let out a long shaking breath and looked over at Sue, who put a hand on her shoulder.

"Come on inside, love." Sue led Ellie back in and made her sit down.

The customer who had followed Sue outside, said, "You're better off without him, love,"

Ellie said, "Thank you. For ... you know."

He smiled. "I have daughters," he said and sat back down to drink his coffee and read his paper as though nothing had interrupted him.

Ellie stared at the table top. There were a few grains of sugar spilled on it. She should get that cleaned up. Yes. She must. But she didn't move.

Sue put a cup of tea in front of Ellie. "Well done, Ellie love. That can't have been easy to do."

Ellie nodded, numbly.

"Do you want to talk about it?"

"Pretend I'm not here," said the customer cheerfully.

That made Ellie snort. In a village this small, the gossip would already be everywhere that Ellie had split up with young Luke who worked at the garage. She unfroze and took the cup of tea in both hands.

"You were right," she said to Sue. "I thought about what you said yesterday and you were right. I am ... was... scared of him. That's not what I want for the rest of my life."

Sue sat down and put a gentle hand on Ellie's arm. "I'm sorry, love. I know it's hard right now, but you really can do so much better than him."

She wasn't so sure about that. She didn't know many men now that she was out of school. But now she was free to do whatever she wanted to ... like go to her best friend's wedding.

"Sue," she said. "If I can afford the ticket, would you give me time off to go to Sophie's wedding?"

Sue laughed. "Of course I will! What's more, I'll even give you a loan of two weeks' wages for you to work off when you get back."

SHE LEFT WORK A LITTLE early, just in case Luke showed up again. She called Sophie on the way. "I split up with Luke," she said, instead of 'hello'.

"Ellie, that's great news," Sophie said. "I'm so proud of you."

Ellie frowned. "You are?"

"He wasn't good to you. You're better off without him."

If that had been the case, why hadn't Sophie tried to persuade her against Luke, earlier? Depressingly, she suspected she wouldn't have listened.

"How are you feeling?" Sophie's voice was cautious and concerned.

She wasn't sure how she was feeling, but she was sure about what she was going to do. "If that train ticket offer is still available, I can come to your wedding. When do you need me to get there?"

Sophie gave a whoop loud enough that Ellie had to move the phone away from her ear. When the noise subsided, she said, "I'm no use to you if I'm deaf in one ear, bird."

"Oh, I won't care. That's the best news I've had all week. Let me call Ash and find out train times and things for you. He's coming from St Pancras. You'll have to get down to London."

"I can do that," she said. She'd never been to London before, but she'd work it out.

Sophie seemed to read her mind. "There's a Megabus from Huddersfield. I'll send you a link to the website." She giggled. "I'm so excited to see you, Ellie!"

"Me too." Happiness rose like a bubble in her chest. She was going to her friend's wedding. The mere thought of it felt like a cloud lifting. "What do I need to bring?"

"Let's see. Tent. Sun cream..." Sophie rattled off a list of things. "It's quite hot. Maybe buy a sun hat."

"And a phrase book," Ellie added.

"Ah, you'll be fine. By the time the wedding arrives, there'll be people from all over the place, so everyone will speak English anyway. It'll be fiiiine."

She had walked almost all the way home before Sophie said, "How's your dad taking it?"

Ellie stopped, one hand on her gate post. "I haven't told him yet. He's ... not going to be happy."

"No," said Sophie. "But just because of what happened with your mum, he can't keep you clapped up in the house."

That didn't stop him from trying though, did it?

"Listen," Sophie added. "Your mum was probably already unhappy with your dad. She needed to get out of the marriage and then she met someone who made her happy. She could have handled it differently, but ... she didn't. You're not her, okay. And tell your dad, I'll make sure you come home to him."

Ellie sighed. "I might have to get you to talk to him," she said. "But I'll try by myself first, okay? Wish me luck. I'm going to need it."

Chapter 5

She didn't tell her father until the night before she left. It seemed easiest that way. The only reason Ellie had a passport at all was because she had once thought she might be able to go on holiday with Luke. After all, he had a passport. She had done it quietly, without telling her father, because she'd known he'd be weird about it. Luke had thought it was funny. In the end, the promised holiday had never materialised and Ellie's passport remained pristine. She'd kept it hidden and pretty much forgotten she even had it. Thankfully, it still had a year left on it before it expired.

Her bag was packed and in her room and everything was ready in case she needed to beat a hasty retreat. She went into the front room where he was sitting, watching telly.

"Dad. I've got something to tell you."

"Eh? What?" He didn't even look away.

"I'm going away for a week."

"With Luke?"

"No. Not with Luke."

There was a silence, where she could see him working things out.

"I'm going to France, for Sophie's wedding. I'll be back next Saturday night."

"No you're not. Luke said you weren't going." He stood up. "Don't be daft."

She ignored the bit about Luke. "But I am," she said, firmly. "Sophie has got me a ticket. I'm catching a bus down to London first thing tomorrow. I will be back in a week." She had to keep telling him that she'd be back because … well, she had to.

"I won't let you," he said, glaring at her. "I didn't spend all these years looking after you for you to bugger off like your mother."

"I'm not Mum!" She was shouting now. "How many times, Dad. I'm not her. I told you I'll come back and I will."

"I can't believe I raised a child that's so ungrateful! I give you everything I've got and you'll just piss off to France," he shouted back. "Oh, it's 'I'll be back next week' now. But what happens when you meet the charming French Lothario? You'll forget all about who's important. Don't blame me if you end up knocked up and alone on the streets of France. It'll serve you bloody right."

"For god's sake! I'm twenty one! You don't get to control where I can and can't go! Did you pull this shit with mum too? Have you ever thought that maybe what happened was YOUR fault? Maybe Mum ran away with a Spaniard because she was running away from you!"

He blanched. Ellie immediately regretted it. "I'm sorry. I didn't mean-"

Her father stepped towards her. "Fine," he snarled. "You go. Don't think I'll be waiting with open arms when you come back. If you come back." He stamped out.

Ellie rolled her eyes. "Where are you going?"

"What do you care?" He shouted over his shoulder and slammed the door on his way out.

Ellie stood in the living room for a moment, listening to the sound of the gate slamming. She sighed and turned off the telly. That had gone better than she'd imagined. She had expected a screaming row. He'd stormed out instead. That was probably a good thing. Probably.

She straightened out the room, picked up her dad's used mug and plate and quietly turned the light off.

THE NEXT MORNING, ELLIE woke up at 4am, before her alarm went off. She checked the time and rolled over. Something dug into her back and she remembered that, in a fit of paranoia, she had slept with her handbag in the bed, so that her passport and bus tickets weren't lying around in case her dad decided to hide them so that she couldn't go.

She lay still and listened. Nothing. She got up, hitched her bag onto her shoulder and pulled her dressing gown on. Cautiously, she unlocked the door.

She tiptoed down the landing to the bathroom and brushed her teeth as quietly as she could. Back in her room, she dressed quickly. Sue was going to give her a lift to the bus station. Her bus was at six o'clock. She checked her documents again and had another quick look in her backpack. She wasn't taking a huge amount of stuff - after all, it was the summer and she was only going for a few days. The thing that weighed the most was her tent, which she had strapped to the base of her bag. Lucky she'd carried this huge backpack before, so she was used to the weight of it.

She placed the bag by the door and went into the kitchen to get herself something to eat. She was just sitting down with a coffee and a couple of slices of bread and butter. There was a small sound from upstairs. She knew he was home. She'd heard him come in and she could see his coat on the hook in the hallway. He clearly wasn't going to come down to say goodbye. Much as she hated leaving things the way they were, going up to talk to him was too much of a risk, this close to leaving. She pulled an old envelope out of the recycling and wrote him a note.

'Dad, I promise, I am coming back. I am just going to France to see my friend. I will call and text you every day. I will be fine. I'll see you next week, I promise you. I love you. Ellie.'

She left the note in the middle of the table, weighed down by a mug. When she heard the car come down the road, she grabbed her jacket, swung her backpack on her back and said 'Bye dad', loudly, from the bottom of the stairs and left.

Sue's boyfriend Jack helped Ellie put her bag in the boot. She got into the car and, as they pulled away, she saw the curtains upstairs twitch and her father's pale face watched her leave.

Sue turned around in the passenger seat. "He'll be okay, love," she said. "I'll keep an eye out for him for you."

Ellie nodded. She was only just realising the enormity of what she had set out to do.

Chapter 6

Ellie checked her phone again and looked up. St Pancras station was enormous. How was she meant to find Ash among all these people? She pulled her bag along behind her until she reached a wall. She checked her phone yet again. Her shoulders and jaw ached with tension. This was her first time in London by herself and she had just made the trip from the coach station, to St Pancras Station on the Underground. She should feel like a rock star, but all she felt was terrified.

Sophie's email said 'Near Cath Kidston, so that you have something nice to look at if he's late.' Ellie scanned the shops until she spotted the familiar red writing on powder blue. Cath Kidston. She clutched her phone tightly and grabbed the handle of her bag again. She tried to head straight for the shop, but she had to keep stopping and letting people pass. No one stopped to let her pass. People tutted at her for getting in their way. Everyone was so bad tempered! Maybe Dad and Luke had a point. Maybe she would have been better staying at home.

At last, she spotted a familiar figure. He was standing, not leaning against a wall or anything, but just standing, his legs either side of a big backpack, head bent as he read on an e-reader.

"Ash!"

He looked up and Ellie nearly collapsed with relief. "It is you, oh thank god."

A smile broke across his face. "Ellie."

The fact that he was pleased to see her, in this horrible, horrible place, was too much. She threw her arms around him and hugged. "I'm so glad to see a familiar face," she said into his shoulder.

Ash didn't move for a few seconds, then patted her back. She felt the awkwardness and let go of him. She took a small step back. "I'm sorry. Am I late?"

"No. No. Plenty of time." He pushed the e-reader into one of the pockets in his cargo trousers. "I've … er… got your ticket. Do you want it?"

She was about to say that he should keep it safe, but then remembered that was what she did when she went places with Luke. She was being independent this week. "Yes please. It was so lucky that you had a spare ticket." Sophie had paid for it. She owed Sophie money now, on top of everything else. Pushing the thought to the back of her mind, she took the ticket he held out and zipped it into the money pouch that Sue had lent her for the journey. It looked ridiculous having a small bag strapped to your waist, but she didn't want her valuable tickets and money to be nicked. She pulled her jacket across so that the pouch was less obvious.

Ash's expression flickered, but he didn't say anything.

Ellie rubbed a hand over her eyes. "London is so … "

"Mad?" he suggested.

She nodded. "I've only been here an hour and I'm already confused."

"It'll be quieter once we go into the Eurostar area." He checked the time. "We can probably go in now, if you like."

She nodded again. Now that she was with someone, she already felt better.

He led the way. Once inside, he left her with the bags and got them two teas. She watched him walking towards her with a lidded cup in each hand. He was tall and slim. He looked different here than he did when she'd last seen him in the pub. Then, he'd been fidgety and uncomfortable in his own skin. Now he seemed altogether more relaxed, as though he belonged. Fleetingly, she thought about how being brown made him stand out in Trewton Royd. Here, where there were people of all sorts of ethnicities around, he fitted in much better.

"When was the last time you were in London?" he said, as he handed her the drink.

"School trip when I was fourteen."

"That's a long time ago. No wonder you're overwhelmed."

She frowned. "I'm not overwhelmed. I got here, didn't I?"

"You did." He looked a little taken aback. "I just thought, if you hadn't been for a while, you managed to navigate the underground for the first time without any trouble. That's pretty impressive."

She eyed him suspiciously, but he didn't appear to be teasing her. If anything, he looked nervous. "Oh," she said. "Thanks."

He gave her a small smile and turned to check the departure board. "We have a bit of time." He settled his bag at his feet and took a sip of his tea. Awkwardness wavered between them. They had to travel all the way to France together and she had just snapped at him when he was just being nice.

"Listen, Ash. I'm sorry I snapped. I didn't mean to. I'm just a bit sensitive right now."

He looked at her, a concerned frown on his face. "Is everything okay?"

"Oh. Yes. Just ... you know. Travelling makes me tense."

"Ah," he said. "I understand."

They stood side by side, awkwardly.

"So, how come Luke's not coming with you?" said Ash, casually.

Ellie turned to stare at him. "I thought you and he didn't get on?" Luke called him Ass for heaven's sake.

"Oh, I'm not complaining," Ash still didn't make eye contact. "I'm just surprised, that's all."

Surprised. Right. Because she had no existence apart from being Luke's girlfriend. "We're not together anymore," she said, tightly. "We split up."

Now he looked at her. Did his eyes just light up?

"That's ... sad," he said. "Are you okay?"

"Yes. I'm fine." Then, because she felt it needed saying, she added, "I dumped him."

"What did he do?" A hint of amusement flashed across his face before he got his expression under control.

"It doesn't matter," she said.

"Well, you can do better than him."

"Why does everyone say that?" said Ellie. "Apart from my Dad, who thinks he's the best thing since sliced bread."

"Probably because it's true. He's a bully. While you're bright and you're nice and you're very pretty."

She drew a sharp breath at that. Was he coming on to her? That was unexpected.

His eyes widened, as though he'd only just realised what he said.

"I'm sorry," he said. "I.... That was creepy. I didn't mean it like that. I mean, you are. All those things. I just." He cleared his throat. "I'll just shut up now."

She could see the redness creeping into his cheeks, glowing through the brown of his skin. Was he blushing? She softened.

"It's okay," she gave him a tiny smile. "It's nice to know that people think of me like that."

"Of course we do."

"We?" she said.

"Me. And other people," he said, quickly. "Everyone. You're a really nice person and Luke's a dickhead."

Ellie shook her head. "He's not that bad," she said. Her gaze moved to the floor. Why was she defending him? Ash was right, Luke was a dickhead, but it still felt disloyal to agree.

She sipped her tea, thoughtfully. Ash too seemed to be deep in thought, or just avoiding eye contact. His hand strayed to the pocket where his e-reader was, as though all he wanted was to get back to his book. It suddenly occurred to her that, for all his apparent confidence, Ash hadn't really changed that much at all. He was still shy and awkward. And he probably didn't want her for a travelling companion. Who would? She was so green. He must feel like he was babysitting.

Oh dear. This was going to be a very awkward journey. Thankfully the tannoy announced their train. "Oh, that's us."

Ash grabbed his bag and pointed towards the platforms. "Come on. Let's get on."

THEY HAD THREE HOURS in Paris. There were so many people! London had been scary, but at least she could read the signs and understand what people were saying. What little French she knew seemed to have fallen out of her head. Ash walked ahead of her, navigating the Metro with relative confidence. They came out of Gare Montparnasse as part of a huge flow of people. She struggled to keep up with him. It was unthinkable that she should lose sight of him and she couldn't exactly hold on to him, so she settled for following him very closely.

When he stopped and she almost walked into him.

"There," he said. "Left luggage."

She looked at where he was pointing and saw that the sign was in English and in French. "That's expensive," she said.

"Yes, but it means we don't have to drag our bags around with us. Let's go and explore for a bit."

She glanced at her watch. "Shouldn't we stay here, until the train is announced?"

"We have three hours, Ellie. Let's go and see the sights."

But what if they missed their train? Or someone picked their pockets and they lost all their money and their train tickets? Or they somehow got involved in one of those terror incidents that happened? Or someone stole their bags out of the left luggage? Ellie tightened her grip on her bag.

Ash's frown deepened.

Ellie braced herself for an argument. "I think we should stay in here," she said, and was pleased to note that her voice barely shook at all.

Ash studied her face for a moment, his dark eyes thoughtful. Then he nodded, slowly. "Okay," he said. "How about ...

we get a coffee just outside." He pointed to the door. "Within sight of the station." He looked at her hand. She followed his gaze and saw that her knuckles had blanched from gripping the handle of her case. She forced herself to loosen her grip.

"And we can take our cases with us," he added. "We can use the money we save to buy a pastry or something."

Ellie looked outside, where the sun was shining on hordes of people. There were hordes of people in here too. At least outside there was sun. "Okay," she said. "Let's do that."

So they ended up at a tiny outdoor table, with bags wedged by their legs, at a cafe round the back of the station. She sat there, watching people going about their business, while Ash, in hesitant French, ordered two hot chocolates and a pastry.

Ellie had only done French to GCSE and she was out of practice, but even she had to wince at how bad Ash's pronunciation was. The waiter was smirking. He must speak English anyway. But she didn't dare say anything. If she did, Ash might ask her to order the stuff and she wasn't sure she'd be able to do it. It was all very well being able to work out the French in her head, but saying it out loud ... that was a different matter entirely!

Ash finally finished ordering and the waiter moved off. He sat back and blew out his cheeks. "That was harder than I thought it was going to be."

Ellie smiled. "I guess you don't have to speak French very often." She shifted position, patting her waist bag to check it was still there.

"Not really," he said. "I tried to listen to some lessons before I came, to see if it came back. Turns out I didn't know much to start with."

"I thought you did really well," she said. At least he'd tried, which was more than she could say for herself. "You must travel a lot. Have you been here before?"

"Once. With my parents. I was about twelve." He grinned. "Dad made us do the tourist thing. All I really remember is having very nice hot chocolates and very sore feet. How about you?"

She shook her head. "I've never been before." She fiddled with the plastic flowers on the table. "I haven't been anywhere outside England since I was about ten." Dad didn't do foreign travel. She understood where he was coming from. In his mind, if they hadn't gone abroad, Mum would never have left them. She hadn't bothered arguing with him about it until that morning. There had always been other things to think about. People went on holiday to Tenerife or Greece and she and Dad could never afford it. Then, she'd met Luke and there had been him to think about. Now, for the first time, she felt bad for not having travelled. She sneaked a glance at Ash, to see if he was judging her.

He was leaning back in his chair, eyes closed, face raised to the sun. He wasn't even thinking about her. Oh. Well, that was probably a good thing. He looked more relaxed now than he'd done on the Eurostar. They hadn't talked much, mainly because she had fallen asleep pretty soon after they left and only woken up when he'd tapped her shoulder to say they were coming into Paris. As she watched, he took a deep breath, making his chest rise and let his breath out in a sigh. When he wasn't buzzing with nervous energy, he was quite attractive. He had strong features and high cheekbones. In the sunshine, his brown skin seemed to glow with health.

The fact that she was noticing any of this seemed wrong. She looked back at her hands and did a quick check again that her bag was still there.

"I think," Ash said, his eyes still closed. "It doesn't matter if you've travelled or not, so long as you've kept an open mind."

"What?"

He raised his head and looked at her. She realised that his eyes weren't black, like she'd originally thought, but very dark brown. In this light, she could see shades of lighter brown in them.

"Travelling to places is great," he said. "But the thing that it teaches you is that there is no right way to do things. People are people and different isn't the same as wrong. You don't have to go to a place to find that out. You can learn that without leaving the house, if you were minded to."

She chewed the side of her lip and considered him. Technically, she'd known him for years, but she realised she knew very little about him. All she could really remember of him was that he read a lot. Sophie liked him, so he must be okay. Luke disliked him, so ... actually, she wasn't sure what that meant. "Did you learn that from reading?" she asked.

Ash blinked. "I guess," he said. "I learned most things from reading books, to be fair." He sat up when the waiter arrived and managed to ask for the bill, assisted mainly by making scribbling gestures with his hand.

"It's a pretty profound thing to get from reading Game of Thrones." Ellie picked up her hot chocolate and blew on it.

"Oh no, I learned that from reading Katie Fforde."

She looked up, sharply. "Don't diss," she said. Once upon a time she'd read a lot of books like that.

"I'm not actually," he said. "I've learned a lot about people in situations other than my own by reading romance. And from reading sci fi and horror and ... everything."

That was something else she remembered. The fact that he seemed to read a very random selection of things.

"I used to read a bit," she said. "But I don't so much now."

"Why not?"

"Luke says reading silly books gives me silly ideas."

His face was one of genuine horror. "You stopped reading because of him?" he said. "That's... awful."

And there it was, the judgement. Of course he thought she was stupid. It was only a matter of time. She looked down. "It was silly of me to-"

"No," he said. "It wasn't silly of you. It was mean of him." He gave her a sudden grin. "It's not too late, though. You can start again. Luke's not here. So why not read the lightest, funniest book you can find and go from there."

"I could, couldn't I?" Luke didn't get to judge her any more. She could do whatever she wanted. The idea made her laugh. "Thanks Ash. I think I'll do that."

He raised his mug of hot chocolate. "To reading."

She clinked her own mug against his. "To reading."

Chapter 7

It was gathering dusk when they finally got to the place they were meant to go. They walked out of the small train station, each dragging their suitcase.

"Where to next?" said Ellie. Her eyes felt dry and she was dying for a cup of tea. She looked around. They were in the car park. Ahead of them was a wide boulevard with pollarded trees and cars parked in a line in the middle. It was warm and everything was bathed in a soft orange glow. Around them, people chatted in French, too fast for her to catch a word. The whole place felt so ... different. She took a small step closer to Ash.

Ash pulled out his folded bit of paper that he'd been consulting at regular intervals along the way. "I think we just get a taxi or something to the house. I mean, we could walk it," he said dubiously.

Someone shouted 'Ellie'. She turned around and spotted a young woman running towards her.

"Sophie!" Oh thank goodness. The place suddenly felt less alien.

"You made it," Sophie gave Ellie a big hug. "Oh, it's so good to see you." She let go of her and stepped across to air kiss Ash's cheek in the European way. "I had to come into the village to get some things, so I thought I'd wait and pick you up too. Come on."

Ellie exchanged a glance with Ash. They didn't need to fork out for a taxi now, so that was good. She picked up her bag and followed Sophie to a small car.

"So, how was your journey?" said Sophie, popping the boot of the car open. As Ellie lifted her bag in, Sophie said, "Was it okay? I know it's your first time travelling."

"It was … fine, really," said Ellie. "I mean, I had Ash to show me how to do stuff."

"It was mainly ordering stuff in terrible French," said Ash. "The rest was just getting on and off trains and being glared at when you get in the way of the locals. You don't need help with that."

Ellie laughed. "I guess not."

They got in, Ash in the back, Ellie in the front with Sophie. Her friend chatted away, keeping up a stream of commentary as she drove on the right like she'd been doing it for years. She had only been in France for a year. Ellie hadn't seen her friend since the summer before and while she couldn't tell exactly what had changed there was something different about Sophie now. Perhaps it was the tan, and her curly hair, always light brown, was now almost blonde. Perhaps it was just the way she seemed to radiate confident happiness. Whatever it was, it suited her.

"A few of the others are already here," Sophie said. "But there's still plenty of space left for two more tents."

"Others?" The sense of relief she'd felt on seeing her friend seeped away.

"Some of Ethan's friends from uni. A few of our friends from the teaching college." Sophie glanced at her. "Don't worry. You'll love them."

"Are they all French?" said Ellie. There was no way she was going to understand a word they said. Ash was trying, but even she could tell his French was rudimentary. She felt so stupid when she didn't understand what people were saying.

"No," said Sophie, peering carefully and turning. "Some are, obviously. There's a couple of Germans, a few Dutch. There's a few more coming tomorrow. One American too."

"Oh," said Ellie.

"I guess I'm going to have to brush up my French pretty fast," said Ash, from the back.

"Oh, most of them speak English," said Sophie. "Apart from the family. Ethan's Grand-mere doesn't. His parents do, of a fashion, but I think they're too shy to try it."

Ellie turned and looked at Ash. This could be a long week. He grinned at her and gave her thumbs up. Ellie turned round and wished she had his cast iron confidence.

They drove over a bridge that crossed a wide river. If she'd needed a reminder that she was in another country, this was it. Houses either side of the wide river had terraces that came out to the water. There was so much soft light. It glinted off the water and gleamed off windows. It was beautiful.

"We'll have to come and explore tomorrow," said Ash, his face pressed against the window.

"I'll show you where the Tourist information place is," said Sophie. "They have a few sights around here. There's a pretty good bus service to most places. Or you might be able to get a lift with the others, if they're going."

A few minutes later, they were in a less populated area. Finally, Sophie pulled into a wide drive that led to what Ellie would have described as a manor house.

"Here we are. Welcome." Sophie beamed at Ellie and opened the boot. Ellie grabbed her bag and gaped at the house, with its blue window shutters that had been thrown open against the ivy clad stone.

"The family used to own a lot of land around here," Sophie said. "But they've sold bits of it off and now all that's left is the house and gardens and few holiday properties in the village." She produced a key from her jeans pocket and let them in through the heavy oak door.

They were ushered inside into a stone flagged hallway. A dark wooden staircase ran up on one side. Evening sunlight slanted in from the windows, marking the hallway in rectangles of light.

"I guess you'd better get your tents up first, so that they're done before it gets dark," Sophie said. "And then I'll introduce you to people."

They walked through the hall, going past a doorway where light spilled out. Sophie called something in French through the doorway as they went past.

Outside, a group of people sat on garden chairs. A trestle table at one side had a collection of beers on it.

"Hi everyone," said Sophie. "These are my friends from England. I'm just going to find them a place to pitch the tents. I'll introduce you guys in a minute."

A chorus of voices shouted 'hello' in a variety of accents.

Beyond the patio was a large expanse of grass. It wasn't a lawn. As far as Ellie could tell, it was a field that led straight to the house. Near the house there were vegetable beds and a greenhouse and at the far edges, there were hedgerows, but other than that, it was all slightly overgrown grass.

"We're leaving the back door open the whole time, so you can access the house if you need the loo or anything from the kitchen." Sophie waved an arm. "Just pick a spot and put up your tents."

"How about here?" said Ash.

It was a small distance away from two other tents.

"Sure," said Ellie.

"I'll leave you guys to it," said Sophie. "I'm helping Juliette cook dinner."

"Okay. See you in a bit," said Ellie. "Who's Juliette?" she whispered to Ash.

"No idea." He put down his huge backpack and pulled out a bag. "This is my tent," he said, looking at it. "Well, Matt's really. He let me borrow it."

"That's fancy," said Ellie. "Looks really light."

"It is. I expect there's instructions on how to set it up. Matt showed me, but I can't really remember."

Ellie's tent was a bit heavier. But then it was a two person tent and not as snazzy as the one Ash had. It wasn't the one she and Sophie had used when they were young. That old tent, heavy and clunky, had finally given up the ghost when one of the tent poles snapped. She had saved up for this one. Luke called it 'their' tent, but really, it was all hers. And Dad's, possibly.

Leaving Ash to sort himself out, she pulled out her tent and laid it out "Ash, can you give us a hand?" she said.

"Of course." He didn't seem to have got very far with his own tent. "If you'll give me a hand with mine."

She looked at the pile of bits. He hadn't even started. "Fine. Let's get this one up and I'll show you how to do yours." She passed him the tent. "Hold this." She fed the relevant rods through the relevant channels. With Ash's help, she had the tent constructed and pegged down within a few minutes.

She put her hands on her hips and looked at Ash's tent. "Have you really never put a tent up before?" It was obvious from the level of instruction he needed.

He gave her a sheepish smile. "No. I'm more of a theory guy. I'm not good with practical stuff."

"How do you mean?" She picked up his tent and tried to work out what went where.

"Give me a text book and a puzzle, and I'm your man. If you want a shelf building ... or, I dunno, to do some sports, you really need someone else."

She passed him a bendy tent pole and showed him how to attach it. Now that she thought of it, she had never seen him in any of the sports teams. She had spent most of her time doing sports. No wonder she'd barely noticed him at school.

"But camping, though," she said. "I thought everyone went camping. What did you do in the summer?"

"Uh ... I went down south to stay with my Aunt. From time to time we went to Spain. Once every few years we went to see the family in Sri Lanka. If not, I just worked. I used to do mornings at the newsagents and then sometimes I did virtual assistant stuff in the evening."

"What's that?"

"I had a few people who needed data logged into spreadsheets and stuff. They had it all in the cloud, so I could log in from home and just do a few hours each night. They paid me for the work done, not the time spent, if you see what I mean. It was boring, but paid okay."

He was good at following instructions. His tent was quite fancy and apparently built to be erected with as little skill as possible, so it took them hardly any time at all to pitch it.

The two tents were pitched at an angle to each other, so that the entrances faced away. That way, they both had a modicum of privacy. Not that you got much privacy camping out in a field.

She stashed her bag inside and stood in front of the tent, looking at the group of people at the top of the garden. "I suppose we'd better go speak to them."

"I guess we should," said Ash. "I'm starving."

"I've got a chocolate bar in my bag," she said. "Want it?"

"Yes please."

She fetched him the chocolate bar, which he broke in half. Ellie took her half and nibbled at it. The longer they hung around here, the less time they'd have with the strangers.

Ash popped the last piece of chocolate in his mouth. "Come on then," he said. "Let's go be sociable."

She followed him reluctantly. If Luke had been here, she'd have slipped her arm through his and let him do the talking. She didn't think she could do that with Ash. She and Ash weren't a couple. They just happened to travel here together. What were the rules for single girls? She had been half of a couple for so long, she really couldn't remember anymore.

Ash took a deep breath, threw her a quick smile, and strode up to the group. Four guys and a girl. Ellie followed along.

"Hi," he said. "Mind if we join you?"

Everyone looked at them. They were all smiling. "Sure. Sure. Of course," said one, in strongly accented English. "There are spare chairs over there. Here. Let me get one for you." He leapt up and went to a stack of folding chairs that was leaning against the side of the house. "We are lucky to have some of the furniture from the neighbours."

He carried a chair back to where Ellie was standing and flipped it open. "For you," he said, with a flourish. "I am Tomas." He held out a hand.

"Um ... I'm Ellie," she said. Her voice was small and high. She swallowed.

"I'm Ash."

Tomas turned to shake Ash's hand. "Welcome. You came from England today?"

"Yes."

They sat down. Tomas introduced them to everyone. Ellie tried to remember their names, but found she couldn't. The woman was called Helene. At least that sounded familiar enough.

"Can I get you a drink?" Tomas said.

"Ah, we haven't had chance to-" Ash began.

"Don't worry. Tomorrow, you can contribute. Right, Helene?"

"Correct," said Helene. On the table beside her were some small glass beakers and a bottle of wine. She poured them a small glass each and passed it down.

Ellie looked at the little glass. It was smaller than she was used to. At home, they used old Nutella glasses. Some even had cartoons on them. It struck her that most people had proper glasses. These people had special little glasses for drinking wine from. Somehow it seemed unbelievably sophisticated.

"That's very kind," Ash said. "Cheers."

There was a chorus of toasts.

"How do you say?" said one of the other guys. "Chin chin?"

Everyone laughed. Ellie felt the muscles in her neck clench. They were laughing at them. She thought of her dad. Had he been right all along? Did all Europeans hate the Brits? She shot a glance as Ash, who didn't seem to be too fussed.

"So," he said. "Have you guys been here for days?"

Tomas seemed keen to talk. He ran through when people had arrived and from where. He asked them about their journey. While they were talking, the others in the group started chatting amongst themselves. Ellie tried to catch what they were saying but she didn't understand a word. It wasn't even French. It made her feel uncomfortable. What if they were talking about her?

Tomas was still chatting, leaning forward so that his blonde head was angled towards Ash. Apparently, he had been watching The Crown on Netflix. Ellie didn't have Netflix. Ash seemed to know a lot about it.

"I didn't know you were a fan?" she said to Ash. The minute she said it, she realised how weird that sounded. Why would she know he was a fan? She didn't know much about him at all, apart from he'd been to the same school as her and Sophie had invited him to this wedding. Oh god. She was surrounded by strangers. The only person she really knew was Sophie. Where was Sophie?

Ash was replying to her.

"What?" she said.

"I said, my mum's a fan. Doesn't stop talking about it. Apparently, Matt Smith is very sexy as Prince Philip and she finds this very disturbing." Ash took a sip of his wine. "Mind you, not half as disturbing as I find that statement."

Tomas laughed. "Well it is very strange after watching Doctor Who."

"You watch Doctor Who?" Ash perked up. He must watch it too.

"How do you feel about the new Doctor? Do you like her?"

"She's alright," said Ash. "I love the northern accent. And that Tim Shaw thing was hilarious."

"I did not understand some of that first episode," Tomas said. "They speak very fast."

"We do," said Ash.

"You sound a little similar, I think."

"We're from Yorkshire," said Ellie, firmly. "She's from Huddersfield. Near us."

"Oh," said Ash. "Do you watch Doctor Who, Ellie? I hadn't thought you would."

She didn't often admit to that. Luke laughed at her for watching a show about aliens. To be fair, she'd started watching it because she fancied Matt Smith. Luke had occasionally put it on because he liked Karen Gillian. Once Karen Gillian left the show, he'd stopped bothering.

Tomas was watching this exchange with interest. "You two ..." he said, gesturing between them with his glass. "You are not a couple?"

"Oh, no," said Ellie. "Just friends."

"Ah," Tomas beamed. "I see." His eyes rested on Ellie's face a fraction of a second longer than they should have. She wished she'd said she and Ash were together now. She didn't want some strange bloke hitting on her. She didn't know any of these people and she was sleeping outside in a tent. By herself. She looked down at the small glass clutched in both hands. Why hadn't she listened to her dad when he warned her about how precarious this all was? What had she been thinking?

Her breath came short. Her heart sped up. The feeling of panic was unfamiliar. She wasn't normally shy. But then again, she wasn't normally alone. She had always had Luke with her. Oh god. Was he right? Did she need him more than she knew?

Someone touched her arm and made her jump.

She looked up to see Ash's worried face. "I'm sorry. I didn't mean to make you jump," he said. "Are you okay?"

Ellie stood up. "I was wondering where Sophie was."

"Shall we go find her?" Ash said. He was still looking at her with a puzzled expression on his face.

"Yes," said Ellie. "I'll go do that."

He came with her, even though she hadn't asked him to. She was glad he had, because when they reached the kitchen, all she could hear was French. Ash knocked and they shuffled in.

The kitchen was big and felt cool, despite the warmth outside. There were windows on the far wall, but it was dark enough that the main light was on.

An older lady stood by the stove, stirring. Sophie was standing at the table, slicing tomatoes. "Oh, Ellie. Hello." She put down her knife. "Got your tent pitched okay?"

"Yes thanks. Can I help?"

"Of course," said Sophie.

"I'm guessing you've got a lot to catch up on," said Ash. "I'll leave you to it." He disappeared back outside.

Ellie washed her hands, ready to help.

Sophie said, "Ellie, this is Juliette, Ethan's mother." She rattled off a counter introduction in French. Ellie heard the words 'Pat's Pantry' and 'patisserie'.

Juliette looked impressed. "Nice to meet you," she said, haltingly. She asked Sophie something.

"Oh yes," said Sophie. "Ellie, you'd be able to help us with some of the nibbles for the wedding, right? We've got a caterer for the main meal, but we're making the nibbles ourselves."

"I'd love to," said Ellie. Having something to do would be nice. Besides, that meant she would be in the kitchen most of the time and didn't have to spend that much time with the other guests. Thank goodness. "So, what can I do?"

Sophie set her to slicing huge tomatoes for a salad. "So, how are you getting on, our Ellie?" she said, grabbing a red onion to slice. "How was travelling with Ash?"

Ellie shrugged. "It was okay. I mean, he's very nice. Can't put up a tent to save his life, but otherwise, lovely." She arranged the slices on the plate Sophie had started. Sophie added a layer of onion rings.

The next tomato was yellow. Ellie stared at it. "I've never seen a yellow tomato that size before. Not in real life, anyway."

Sophie laughed. "I picked them up from the market. They're delicious." She carried on slicing. "Wait a bit before doing another layer of tomato. I need to slice some mozzarella."

Ellie concentrated on slicing. She felt better now that she was in the familiar environment of a kitchen. It reminded her a little of Sue's warm bakery. The idea of going outside, to hang around with strangers, still worried her. She hoped Ash was okay. Dad had said that foreigners always wanted something, especially if they were being nice. The thought of her dad was a small punch in the gut. He had been so angry with her. Even though she'd texted him when she'd arrived at the station, he hadn't replied. What he never spoke to her again? What had she done?

Sophie was saying something to her. She looked up. "Hmm?"

"I said, I'll get you a plate to put the slices on ..." Sophie frowned. "What's wrong? You look sad."

She started to say she was fine, but the words didn't come. "I'm ... scared, Soph."

"Oh, honey, why?"

"I've never been this far away from Trewton before." Her mind flitted to that ill-fated holiday when she was a child. "Not by myself anyway. And I miss home. I miss Dad. And I miss Luke."

Sophie carefully put her knife down. "Luke? Seriously?"

"Why do you do that? If he was so bad, why didn't you say something earlier?"

Sophie sucked in her lip. "Because ..." she said. "I didn't see it at first. You were so happy. He was popular and he seemed to be genuinely into you and as far as I know, he's not cheated on you... so I thought it would be okay. But whenever I've seen you two together lately, you've been more and more subdued and he's been more and more domineering. He's always telling you your opinion is rubbish. He's always putting you down ... it's like he left school and changed into a different person. One that just kept the bad traits of himself."

Ellie blinked. Sophie wasn't wrong. Luke had changed. It had happened so gradually, she hadn't really noticed until it was too late.

"I'm so proud of you for standing up to him, Ellie." Sophie laid a hand on her arm. "It can't have been easy."

Tears rose in her eyes. "It's not."

"I know, love," said Sophie gently.

"And dad was furious with me for coming." Ellie wiped her eyes with the back of her hand. Juliette appeared with a paper towel and handed it to her.

Ellie murmured her thanks.

"You know he's just frightened, right?" said Sophie. "He thinks you'll leave him too."

Ellie sniffed. "I texted him to say I got here safely, but he didn't reply."

"He'll have read it, though," said Sophie. "Just keep in touch regularly, so that he doesn't worry."

"He was livid when I told him I'd split up with Luke. He said I'd never find a man again."

Sophie sighed. "I love your dad to bits, but he doesn't half have some funny ideas." She shook her head. "He likes Luke because it means nothing will change. If you married Luke, you'd still pop by to see him and you'd all still have tea together on a Wednesday and go to the pub quiz on a Friday. Life would carry on the same way it always did. It would be so easy for him."

Ellie considered this. Sophie had a point. "How did you get so wise all of a sudden?" she said.

"I got out of Trewton," said Sophie. "I love that place, but I'd have gone mad if I had to stay there. I know you're happy there, but I really needed out."

Juliette said something in French. Sophie replied. Even without any understanding of the language, Ellie could tell that Juliette was asking if Sophie wanted her to finish the cooking by herself.

"Sorry," she said. "I'm interfering with your cooking. Here. Let me finish up."

Sophie nodded. "We'll talk again later, yeah?"

"Yeah."

"I'm glad you're here."

Ellie smiled and selected another tomato.

They worked together in silence for a few minutes. It was soothing being in this room, surrounded by kitchen noises. Every so often a shout of laughter would drift in from outside. Juliette and Sophie occasionally spoke to each other. Ellie finished cutting the tomatoes and layered the tomato, onion and mozzarella. Sophie handed her a jar of homemade pesto, which she drizzled on it. It looked and smelled wonderful.

There was a burst of noise from the outside. Sophie's head shot up to listen. "Ethan's back," she said.

Ellie had always suspected that Sophie had met the real thing in Ethan. Now, seeing the way her friend's whole body seemed to light up at the thought of him being home, there was no doubt that Sophie had found the one for her. She looked over at Juliette and saw the fondness of the smile she threw at Sophie. Clearly, Juliette thought her son had chosen well. Ellie was glad to see that at least one of them was doing well in the romance stakes.

Chapter 8

The dinner that Ellie helped Sophie and Juliette cook was an enormous vat of pasta with ragu complemented by two big platters of salad. When they got outside, the rest of the group had set up two tables and set chairs around it. Conversations carried on as people passed plates down and handed out cutlery. It was noisy and overwhelming. So when Ash set a chair down next to his own, Ellie gratefully grabbed it. Once they'd sat down, the conversations switched to predominantly English. It appeared that not everyone spoke German and not everyone spoke French, but almost everyone spoke some English. Ethan, tall and handsome with his light brown hair and strong jawline, sat next to Sophie and translated for his parents.

Although the food was simple, it was delicious. Ethan's father poured wine for everyone. As the red wine did its work, Ellie relaxed a bit. Understanding what was being said made such a difference. When the evening turned to night, Ethan produced some LED lanterns which were placed on the table.

By now, Ellie was feeling so tired, she could barely keep her eyes open.

"So, what will you do tomorrow?" Tomas asked her.

She stifled a yawn. "I don't know. I hadn't really planned that far." She looked at Ash for support.

"There's the Dordogne," Ash said. "We could go see that. Maybe ride a boat down it."

"We are thinking of going there, also," said Tomas. "Helene," he called. "Do we have room in the car for two more persons?"

Helene was a tall woman, with glasses and short brown hair. She had an ageless quality about her. Even though, since she was Ethan's university friend, she must have been around the same age as them, she looked somehow more sophisticated. Helene counted silently on her hand. "Between my car and Peiter's, yes. We can fit two more." Her gaze searched out Ash. "Are you joining us tomorrow?"

"They would like to do the canoe ride down the river," Tomas supplied. "We were thinking that was a good idea, so why not?"

"Very good," said Helene. "Come join us."

Helene was looking at Ash with a speculative gleam in her eye. He didn't seem to have noticed. "That would be great," he said.

Ellie smiled and murmured, "You're very kind."

"Sure," said Helene, nodding to her, as though she'd only just noticed her for the first time. "The more the merrier."

The conversation moved on, but Ellie was so tired, she really couldn't stay up any longer. "I'm going to call it a night," she said.

Ash looked uncertain, as though he didn't know how to react. "Will you be okay getting back to the tent?" he said.

"I have a flashlight on my phone."

She said good night to everyone and headed back to her tent by the light of the lamp. It was pleasantly cool now. Voices and laughter drifted up from the group in the garden. She located her wash bag and headed back into the house to use the bathroom. As she passed, she noticed that now that people had switched back to conversations in smaller groups, it sounded like they were speaking mainly French and German again.

While everyone was outside, the house itself was quiet. The warmth from before had hung around and the kitchen smelled faintly of pesto as she walked past it. Her footsteps felt loud on the stone floor. Once again, she was overwhelmed with how different it all was. She had been on holiday to all manner of places in England, but this felt so much more different to all of them.

Tension had tied painful knots in her shoulders. She felt out of balance and vulnerable. This wasn't as much fun as she'd hoped it would be.

A guffaw of laughter drifted in from outside. Her breath caught. What if they were laughing at her? She shook her head. No, that was silly. Sophie wouldn't let anyone be mean to her. Neither would Ash. She hadn't known him for long, not properly, but on the train journey there, she felt she'd got to know him. He was friendly and kind and, if she were looking, she'd have said he was good looking. But of course, she wasn't looking. Because it was too soon.

She brushed her teeth and walked back outside, with her towel bundled in her arms. She waved to Sophie as she passed. Sophie, tucked in the curve of Ethan's arm, blew her a kiss in return. Someone stood up and came over. She clutched her things even closer.

"Want me to walk you back to the tent?" It was Ash.

Ellie relaxed a fraction. "Thank you. That would be nice."

He brought a torch with him, so she saved her phone battery. "How are you doing? Are you okay?" he said, overly casual.

"I'm fine, why are you asking?"

She couldn't see him in the dark, but she could feel the grimace. "Sophie asked me to check," he said.

Ellie gave a soft laugh. "Of course she did."

"Are you okay with going out with Tomas and Helene tomorrow?"

"I guess so," she said, cautiously. "It was nice of them to offer us a lift."

"Yes, it was."

There was an uncomfortable silence. She wondered if she should mention that she thought Helene fancied him. No. Maybe not.

They reached Ellie's tent and stopped. He held the torch for her while she unzipped the tent and threw her stuff inside. Ash turned the torch to the ground, so that she wasn't dazzled. Her eyes slowly adjusted to the lower level of light. She crawled into the tent and sat down, looking out.

"Can I ask you something?" Ash said. He hunkered down outside the tent, so they were on a level.

"Sure."

"I get the impression you don't like them much." He nodded towards the group still sitting on the patio. "I don't get why. They're nice enough."

"I don't have anything in common with them. And I don't understand them half the time."

"Their English is very good."

"But they keep speaking in German or French."

Ash shrugged. "Only when they're talking to each other. When they talk to us it's only bits here and there, when they've forgotten a word or something. It's natural. Why does it bother you so much?"

"I don't know," she said. "Maybe they're talking about us?"

"Or ... maybe they're not. I'm sure we're not that interesting."

Ellie pressed the heels of her palms to her eyes. "They're just so ... foreign."

She sensed, rather than saw, the change in him. "How so?" His voice was tense now.

"They're just different, okay." She dropped her hands.

"And you don't like them because they're 'foreign'?" He made an air quotes sign. There was something about his tone of voice that scared her. She couldn't place it. Anger? Frustration?

Worried now, she didn't reply. She didn't want to get into an argument with him. He was the only person here, apart from Sophie, whom she could rely on.

"And what about me?" Ash said. "Do you not trust me either? Seeing as I'm foreign."

What was he talking about? "Of course I trust you. You're not foreign."

"Wh-?" He made a noise with his throat. "I'm not even the same colour as you. How do you figure I'm less foreign than they are?"

"Because ..." She didn't know why. She had stopped noticing that he was brown. She noticed the smile, the eyes, the kindness, but the brownness... not really. Besides, her mum had always told her that people were all the same on the inside and it had stuck with her. "Because I know you," she said weakly. She hoped that was the right answer.

"Do you think, maybe, instead of being suspicious and prickly, if you relaxed a little and got to know the others, you might find them less scary? Less foreign." His voice was still tight, as though he was reining in what he actually wanted to say. He looked away at the house in the distance.

"I ... I'll try." She tilted her head. "Ash, why are you being so strange about it?"

"Because, Ellie, all my life I've been 'foreign' in my own home town. Because your boyfriend and his friends ... your friends ... were always there with a handy jibe about 'chocolate skin' or 'smells of curry' or 'marrying your cousins'. All my life. And now you tell me that I'm not foreign to you because I'm another Brit abroad." He picked up the torch again and stood up. "It's ... It's a sensitive subject, okay?"

"I'm sorry. I didn't think-"

"No. I know. I'm going to get a drink. Good night." He stomped off without bothering to hear her reply.

Once inside her tent, Ellie wrapped her arms around her knees, making herself as small as possible. She felt like she'd been told off and needed to make amends. Except, she needed to work out what she was apologising for. She was sure she'd never said any of those things to anyone. But she'd heard it often enough from Luke and from her own father, especially after Mum left. What had she done then? She didn't have to think too hard to know that the answer was nothing. She had done nothing to stop them. She knew not to do it herself, but she'd done nothing to step in and stop other people being racist or bullying, because doing something would have put her into conflict with Luke, or Dad and she didn't ever do that.

She liked Ash. He was kind and sweet. A little clueless at times, like with putting up the tent. It was quite nice to be more competent than him. It was also nice that he didn't seem to mind that she knew more than him about it. There were times with Luke when they'd be doing a pub quiz or chatting to someone else when Ellie had known that Luke's assertion was wrong and she'd never said anything. She just went along with it because contradicting Luke just led to sulking and grousing and she didn't have the energy for that.

Sophie said that Luke had held Ellie back. Is that what she'd meant?

She sighed. That didn't bring her any closer to working out what to do about Ash. Was he calling her racist? Did he have a point? Was she so against people like Helene and Tomas because she thought that was how she was supposed to feel? It was a sobering thought that she might be that gullible ... but she always went along with what Luke wanted and before that, with what her father wanted. She turned her phone on again and checked for messages. Still none. Ellie sighed. By the light of her phone, she got changed and snuggled down into her sleeping bag.

An owl hooted in the distance. In the patio behind the house, figures sat around drinking wine and laughing. Ash would be one of them. So would Sophie. If they could get on with these people, why couldn't she?

Chapter 9

The first thing Ellie did when she woke up was to check her phone to see if her dad had replied to her text. Or her What'sApp message. She tried calling, cost be damned, but it went to answerphone again. She left another message to say she was fine and she could hear the brittle cheeriness in her voice. She hung up and checked all her messages again. Her WhatsApp message had two ticks on it, which meant he'd seen it. He was just sulking. Oh great.

She sighed and turned off her data signal. It cost so much to use roaming data on her contract that she had to be careful with how often she turned it on.

She quickly got dressed, pulling on jeans and a clean t-shirt before she crawled out of the tent. It was still quite early and no one else seemed to be up. She pulled on her trainers, grabbed her stuff and went to use the bathroom. The tents, spaced well apart, were all quiet. The grass was dewy underfoot and, although it was light, it wasn't warm yet. Ellie turned the handle on the door, which was, as Sophie had said, open.

In contrast to the outside, there was movement in the house. After brushing her teeth, Ellie came out into the hallway to find the front door open. Juliette, Ethan's mother, came in carrying a box covered with paper. Instinctively, Ellie leapt forward to get the door for her. She got a nod and 'merci'. Ellie peeped out of the front door, just in time to see a van with what looked like a baker's logo painted on it, pulling out into the road. She closed the door carefully and followed the smell of fresh bread into the kitchen.

"Is that breakfast?" she asked. Her stomach growled.

Juliette said something in French, then, when Ellie didn't understand, waved her hands in a big circle. "All."

"Oh, that's breakfast for everyone," she gestured with her hands, mimicking eating. "All out there?"

She went further into the kitchen, pulled in by the smell. Juliette took the paper cover off the box and pulled out a baguette, which she broke in half and passed a half to Ellie. When she moved away, Ellie grabbed the paper cover and put it back over the loaves. She found a warm spot by the stove and moved the box closer. "To keep them warm," she said to Juliette. "Er... chaud."

Between broken French, broken English and a lot of hand gestures, she ended up having breakfast with Juliette. Warm bread, butter and jam with freshly made coffee. It was delicious. When Ethan sauntered in, the two women were sitting companionably at opposite sides of the table, eating.

He joined them, switching effortlessly between the two languages. Ellie felt a stab of envy. If only she could speak more than one language.

The sounds of activity outside grew louder. Juliette said something in French, which Ellie understood to mean 'we should get breakfast set up'. So she said, "Let me just go put my stuff in my tent and I'll be back to help you set up."

Ethan gave her a surprised look and nodded.

Ellie sped off, threw her towel and wash bag into her tent and ran back. She and Ethan put the trestle tables out. They carried out bread, butter, jam, Nutella, cheese, ham and selection of fruit out to put on the table. People drifted down, some awake and fully dressed, others wearing jumpers over pyjamas and clearly half asleep. There wasn't much conversation to start with as the coffee pot was passed round. Somehow, it seemed more companionable this morning. Difficulty getting started in the morning must be a universal leveller.

Ellie was sitting down with a second mug of coffee by the time Ash showed up.

"Morning," he said, cautiously, as though he wasn't sure what sort of a reception he'd get.

She smiled. "Morning."

He pulled a chair over and sat down next to her. "Um... listen, I'm sorry I got bent out of shape yesterday..." he said.

"And I'm sorry I was so insensitive. You were right. I was being ... closed minded." She thought about how she and Juliette had sat together in the kitchen, with no common language between them. "I should try harder. It's my fault I'm rubbish with languages, not anyone else's."

He nodded, his expression one of massive relief. "Great," he said. He helped himself to some bread and spread a generous layer of Nutella on it. "Still okay to go to the river with the others today?"

"Sure." She watched him take a banana and add it to the bread, mashing it into the chocolate spread. "What are you doing?"

"Banana and chocolate sandwich," he said, as though he expected her to have heard of it. "Don't tell me you've never tried it?"

She shook her head. "Looks disgusting."

"Oh, you haven't lived. Here, try it." He tried to tear off a piece. It was very messy. "I didn't think that through," he said, licking Nutella off his fingers. "Honestly, it's the best thing in the world. You should try it." He found more chocolate on his wrist. "Ugh."

She laughed. "You look like a five year old."

"But a five year old with a Nutella sandwich," he said. "I'm okay with that."

She laughed again and passed him a paper napkin. He gave her a cheeky grin. "Thanks."

He was one of the ones in pyjamas and a jumper. His hair was sticking out in all directions and he had a shadow of stubble. She watched him take a big bite from the sandwich and close his eyes in sheer enjoyment. His pleasure at his ridiculous sandwich made her smile too.

She liked Ash. If she was honest, maybe she liked him a little too much. It was too soon to be noticing anyone else. She had only just split up with a man she'd been going out with for four years. There should be a period of quiet after something as big as that. She would have to take care and not get too attached to Ash. She was only here for a week. It should be safe enough.

"SO, HOW DO YOU KNOW Sophie?"

They were in Tomas's car. Ash in the front passenger seat, Helene and Ellie in the back. Despite her promise to try harder, Ellie was still desperately intimidated by the others. She had tried looking out of the window, in the hope that she'd put Helene off talking to her. It had worked for a while, giving her the chance to listen without having to speak.

So far she'd found out that Tomas didn't much like his job, but it was a step in the right direction. Helene and Tomas were friends of Ethan's from his undergraduate studies; and that Helene was doing a PhD in something clever that she explained, but Ellie didn't fully understand. Ash was asking them interested questions. Ellie felt completely outclassed. She hadn't even done A-levels. She just had vocational qualifications in food hygiene, service and basic business skills.

When she didn't answer, Helene said, "Ellie? How do you know Sophie?"

"We were in the same class at school," said Ellie, softly. "We were best friends."

"And you, Ash. You were in the same school, also?"

Ash twisted round in his seat. "Yes, Sophie and I were in physics together. I don't think you and I had any classes together, did we, Ellie? We weren't in the same form."

"No."

"But you have not finished your undergraduate studies yet, while Sophie has. How is this possible?" Helene asked Ash.

"I worked for a year," said Ash. "I needed to earn money to help with my fees and living expenses."

Ellie frowned. She hadn't really thought about that before. Ash should have gone off to uni at the same time as Sophie, but he had been around, working weekends in the cornershop for a whole year. He must have done something else during the week. It hadn't even occurred to her to wonder what that might have been. Luke had always teased Ash for living off his parents' money and Ellie had assumed he was right. But it seemed that

Ash wasn't rich. Luke had just assumed he was and harassed him.

There followed some discussion about how English schools worked and how A levels compared to the International Baccalaureate. Ellie had nothing to contribute to the conversation. She shrank into her seat and tried not to be intimidated even more.

THEY HIRED CANADIAN style canoes. Ellie shared with Ash while Helene and Tomas shared the other. The guide took them and the canoes upstream. The car was left at the office downstream so that they could retrieve it on their return.

"Shall I go in the back?" she said. "I can steer." She didn't particularly like doing it, but she was probably going to do a better job than someone who'd never done it before.

Ash grinned. "This is one outdoorsy thing I have done before."

"In that case, I'll go in the front." She stepped in and found the paddle.

Ash pushed the canoe off the sloping beach and jumped in as it slid into the water. Ellie, looking over her shoulder, said, "Nicely done."

He looked so pleased with himself that she couldn't help smiling. She turned back around and began paddling.

The river was wide and meandered slowly through a deep valley. The slopes on either side had houses and villages nestled under vertical rock faces. Here and there a private jetty impinged into the river. It was beautiful. After a while, when Ash had got the hang of steering, Ellie put down her paddle and just sat as the canoe drifted. The sun warmed her shoulders. It felt ... like summer should feel.

"Ellie," Ash said. "Look up there."

A castle, dark grey and majestic, perched high up on the side.

"Oh my god, that's amazing!" Ellie pulled her phone out of her dry bag and took a photo. It was hard to do the view justice. "Ash, could you take a photo with me in it?"

She passed the camera back to him and posed, pointing goofily at the castle. The phone clicked.

"It's so beautiful," Ellie said with a sigh. "And to think all this was here all this time and I didn't even know. Can you imagine?" She turned and looked back at him. The camera clicked again.

Ash handed her phone back to her. "Beautiful," he agreed.

She resisted the urge to check the photos there and then. She put the phone back in the dry bag to keep it safe. With her paddle resting on her knees, she leaned back and looked up at the walls of the valley. "I used to think there was nowhere as beautiful as Yorkshire," she said, quietly.

"And now?"

"I think maybe there are some places that come close."

He laughed out loud. Ellie noticed that he had a very nice laugh. Deep and infectious. Something else that had been around all this time and she hadn't noticed. The more she got to know Ash, the more she liked him. How on earth had she not noticed anything about him before? An image of Luke popped into her mind and she felt guilty.

She shook her head and picked up the paddle. A little bit of light seemed to have leached out of the day.

They carried on down the river. It wasn't exactly quiet, there were too many crafts on the river for that, but it was relaxing. Occasionally, she would point something out to Ash, or he to her. Ellie felt the knots in her shoulders loosening, just a little bit.

It was meant to be just over an hour, but it was over far too soon.

"There." Ash pointed towards the huge banner that told them where they needed to pull in to return the canoes. Ellie felt her mood drop. It had been wonderfully tranquil floating down the river, admiring the view. Now they would have to meet up with the others and she would have to keep up with the conversation and struggle to think of things to say.

Her apprehension must have shown on her face, because, as they moored the boat and followed the others up the steps to the street, Ash nudged her. "Relax," he whispered. "They're just people."

"It's alright for you, you're clever and at uni. I don't have anything in common with them."

"Bet you do," said Ash. "We just have to figure out what that is."

She wished she shared his optimism. They handed in their life jackets and the emptied dry bags and set off into the nearby town. Ellie followed the others up the steep streets, until Tomas suggested lunch at a small restaurant.

Before long, they were seated at a table on a little balcony that looked over the street. The angle of the street meant that a lot of higher shops and streets were clearly visible. They were each given a small menu with three main course options. Underneath each option, in small letters was an English translation.

"I am starving," said Tomas.

Ellie ordered the cassoulet, partly out of curiosity. From her seat, she could see the entrance to the restaurant, which had a takeaway section. People came in off the street and took out food in polystyrene containers or, in the case of the soup, a cup with a lid. It seemed a horribly mundane thing to happen in such a glorious holiday town.

Helene turned to see what Ellie was staring at. "You are watching the takeaways?" she asked, turning back.

Startled, Ellie switched her focus. "I was just wondering how that could work back at home."

Helene's quizzical expression made Ellie add, "I work in a bakery. We sell sandwiches, but more often people come and buy a loaf of bread or a whole cake to take home."

"You are a baker!" Helene's expression brightened up. "What sort of things do you bake? Artisan or industrial?"

"Er... Sue makes everything herself, so artisan." Ellie flushed. She wasn't even sure that was the right term for what they did. "Sue is the baker. Not me. I just ... help."

"They sell the most amazing cinnamon buns," Ash added. He turned to Ellie, his expression hopeful. "Do you know how to make those?"

Ellie shook her head. "Those are Sue's speciality." She spotted the disappointment in his expression and added, "I help with the biscuits and cakes. I'm getting pretty good at scones." Now she thought about it, she had helped make quite a number of the things that Sue sold. Even though she had started out as serving staff, when the shop was quiet, she had wandered into the back and offered to help. With time, when things were busy, Sue had given her extra hours to help with the baking. She had been picking up skills without even realising it.

"I am very interested in baking," Helene said, wistfully. "But whatever I try, I always manage to mess things up. Or, even if I do everything exactly as the recipe shows - it just does not look like it should. I am very jealous."

Ellie stared at her. How could Helene with her rock solid confidence and PhD work be jealous of her? That didn't seem possible.

"Can you make bread?" said Helene, suddenly.

That, she knew how to do, so she said yes.

"Ah," said Helene. "I can never get it to rise properly."

"I had that problem when I tried to make bread at home," said Ellie. "Turned out the place I was leaving them to prove wasn't warm enough."

Helene frowned. "I wonder if that is my problem also."

Before she knew it, Ellie was having a very involved discussion with Helene about baking and cake decorating. They stopped talking when their meal arrived. As he bent his head to his meal, Ash caught her eye and smiled. He had been right. She did have something in common with Helene. More to the point, it was something that she was actually good at.

Chapter 10

They got back in the afternoon and all sat on the grass, Ash in the shadow cast by the house, the others in the sun. Ellie checked her phone for messages from her dad. Nothing. She risked burning money on her data connection to see if there was anything on her social media, even though dad didn't do social media. Finally, in exasperation, she texted her aunt Jane. She put her phone face down on her lap and leaned back on her arms, letting the sun fall on her face and neck.

Not far away, Helene finished typing furiously on her phone and sighed. "Hey Ash," she said. "Why not join us in the sun?"

Ash looked up from his e-reader. "No thanks. I don't need to work on my tan."

There was a second or two of silence and Helene laughed. "No. I guess not." She walked over and sat down at the edge of the shade. "What are you reading?"

He told her.

"Do you like crime?" She sounded interested. Ellie felt a small pinch of emotion and couldn't figure out what it was. She couldn't be jealous, surely? Ash was just her friend, she didn't have any claim over him. So what if Helene wanted to talk to him? She tried to ignore them, but her attention kept drifting towards the conversation where Ash was telling Helene he read across a range of genres.

"Sci Fi?" she asked.

"I've read a bit. Mostly the older stuff. Some Sci Fi romance and space opera - the library had a lot of that."

Helene laughed. "Sci Fi romance? I bet you didn't read regular romance."

Ash shrugged. "Sure."

"No way, really?"

Ash put his e-reader down and looked interested. "Why are you surprised? It's a wide ranging and popular genre. Have you read much of it?"

Helene frowned. "No. I confess I have not."

"Well then," said Ash.

She gave another little laugh. "I take your point. I shall read some before I pass judgement." She leaned towards him.

Ash grinned at her. "You might enjoy it. My ex read a lot of it. Sometimes she would recommend books to me. We were never short of things to talk about."

"Oh?" Helene looked at him, meaningfully.

Ash held her gaze, his expression neutral.

Ellie felt another twist of ... oh, of course it was jealousy. She knew there was another level of conversation going on under the surface of the audible one and it was annoying her.

"I see," said Helene. "I am sure that was good fun. The couple that reads sex scenes together, does well together, yes?"

Ash raised his eyebrows. "Not all romances have sex scenes," he said. "But yes, it was very ... educational, at times."

At this Helene threw back her head and laughed, properly. Ellie felt like she'd missed the joke. She pretended to be engrossed in her phone.

"Why are you single?" said Helene, suddenly.

"You're very blunt," said Ash. Ellie could hear the smile in his voice.

"I do not see the point of being any other way." Helene laughed. She was definitely flirting with him.

"That seems like a sensible way to do things," said Ash. Was he flirting back? Ellie couldn't be sure.

"You didn't answer my question. If you are so ... knowledgeable and you are quite attractive, why did you break up with your girlfriend?"

"Ah..." Ash's laugh sounded rushed and embarrassed. "Well, actually she broke up with me. Her ex-boyfriend turned up and told her he wasn't over her ... and it turned out she wasn't over him either."

"Oh," said Helene. "Last in first out. I am sorry. Was that long ago?"

"A few months," he said. "Not very long ago, really."

No wonder he had been reluctant to talk about it when Ellie had asked on the train ride down. What was it with Helene that meant he felt he could talk about it now? Was he interested in her? There was a weighty silence. Ellie didn't dare look up.

"I am ... not really ready to see anyone else yet, I think." Ash said, quietly.

Helene said, "Hmm." There was another beat of silence, before Helene said, "I am going to get a drink. Do you want something?"

"No, I'm good thanks."

Ellie stared at the blank face of her phone and tracked Helene's movements as she walked to the house. Why did she feel so much relief? She liked Ash, but she didn't want him for herself. Did she? She finally sneaked a glance at him and found him staring at her. He flushed a little and smiled at her.

"I think she likes you," she said.

"Ha. Not really," said Ash. He looked back to his book. "Besides, she's not my type."

Did she dare ask what his type was? Did she definitely want to know? Before she could figure out the answer, Sophie came bounding out of the house.

"Hello, you lot," Sophie said. "How was the river?"

They told her about their day. Finally Sophie said, "I need a volunteer to help with cooking tonight's dinner."

Ellie was on her feet in a flash. "I'm happy to help," she said.

"Brilliant," said Sophie. "I had hoped you would." She linked her arm through Ellie's, a familiar gesture from years ago. "You guys," Sophie said, pointing a finger at Ash and Tomas, "Can wash up."

"Happy to," said Ash.

Ellie went back to the house with Sophie, happy to have a few minutes with someone she knew how to talk to. Juliette was in the kitchen again. Ellie muttered 'bonsoir' to her and Juliette gave her a gentle smile.

They were making pasta with tomato sauce again. When Ellie commented that it was more Italian than French, Sophie pointed out that it was also quick and easy when feeding a crowd. "There are more people coming tomorrow," she said. "We'll have to set up a rota or some sort for helpers."

"We can't keep eating your food without paying something," said Ellie. "Maybe you could do a collection box so that people can put some money towards the food."

"Okay." Sophie pulled a notebook out of her jeans pocket and scribbled something down. "Actually, Ellie, there was something I wanted to talk to you about."

Ellie raised her eyebrows, apprehensive. Was she going to get another lecture about all the things she was doing wrong in life?

"It was more a favour, actually," Sophie said.

Ellie relaxed a fraction. Doing favours for Sophie was hardly a problem. "Oh, of course."

"You haven't heard what it is yet."

Fair point. She pretended to brace herself. "Go on then, tell me."

"I wanted us to make some amuse bouche that were English, to give out at the start of the wedding party. Do you think you could do that? A few hundred of each. Small things."

Ellie frowned. "Like what?"

"I don't know. I thought maybe small squares of cake or something." She gestured with her hands, giving the impression of something about one inch square.

Ellie gave it some thought, her own hands, automatically mimicking Sophie's sizing. "What ... like scones? Little ones."

"Oh yes, little scones would be amazing. They'd be proper British," said Sophie, delighted. "We could put cream and jam on them. Anything else? We'd all help you, obviously."

"It'd have to be fairly solid to hold together," said Ellie, thoughtfully. Crumble was too crumbly... custard tarts, maybe, but they'd need loads of baking trays... "How about, squares of bread and butter pudding. If I make it not too squishy, we could cut it into squares."

"I love bread and butter pudding!"

"I know." Ellie laughed. "I haven't forgotten."

Sophie clapped her hands. "This is brilliant."

"I could have made mini Victoria sponges, but we'd need a load of trays with smallish moulds in them."

"Could be tricky," said Sophie.

Juliette, who clearly understood more English than she could speak, said something to Sophie, who brightened up.

"Apparently," she said to Ellie. "The big pans we're using and the baking trays are all hired from a local catering firm. They also hire out specialist cake tins." She checked something with Juliette.

Ellie watched them talking. Sophie's French seemed fluent, but when she watched closely, she could see where her friend hesitated or paused to think of the right word. Eventually, Sophie said, "If we can find you the trays, can you make Victoria sponges?"

"You know I'd love to!"

Sophie gave her a tight squeeze. "I love you, you know that, right?"

Ellie hugged her friend back. "I miss having you around, bird."

"I miss you too."

"But ... hot Frenchman, huh?"

"Yeah, hot Frenchman." Sophie shrugged and spread out her hands. "What can you do?"

Chapter 11

The next day, Ash was trying to convince Ellie she should come with him to see an old church with the others, when Ethan came up and said, "Ellie, my mother says she has the trays you wanted …?" He looked puzzled.

"Oh brilliant," said Ellie.

"Trays?" Ash looked at Ethan, who shrugged.

"I don't know either," said Ethan. "Maman said you'd know what I meant. What's going on?"

"Sophie asked if I'd make some mini English puddings for the wedding. As sweet canapes."

Ethan's expression cleared. "Oh yes! She did mention that to me. Are you going to do it? That would be brilliant."

"I can do it today, if that's convenient for your mum," said Ellie, half rising.

"I think it is," said Ethan. "But finish your coffee first!"

Ash cast a glance as Tomas and Helene, who were poring over their guidebook, and turned back to Ellie. "Do you want some help?"

He clearly wanted to go with the others. Ellie felt another punch of jealousy, stronger now. She did need some help, but she didn't want to keep him at the house if he wanted to go and explore. Ash, she realised, liked learning new things. "I'll be fine," she said.

He hesitated, eyes fixed on her. He was worried about leaving her, even though he clearly wanted to go. That was so sweet. Something in her melted. "Go on," she said, gently. "I'll be fine. Sophie will be here."

She didn't know that Sophie would actually be there. The bride-to-be was always busy.

But Sophie did turn up, not long after the others had left, with bags full of ingredients. Ellie had both Sophie and Juliette to help her. She showed Juliette what she needed to do and the three of them made bread and butter pudding. Ellie tweaked her recipe to make the pudding less runny - it had to hold together so that it could be cut into firm squares. Juliette was astounded by the new way to use up bread and kept asking questions, which Sophie had to translate. As they went along, Sophie and Juliette taught Ellie names for things in French. Her baking related vocabulary increased massively.

But the best thing about the day was spending time with Sophie. Ever since Ellie had been assigned to show the new girl, Sophie, around the school, they had been friends. On a superficial level, they had little in common. Ellie had played sports, been good at art and was popular. Sophie had been skinny, into science and scrappy. Yet somehow, their friendship had worked and solidified through long summers hiking in the moors and taking a sailing course provided for free by a charity. As they grew older, their school lives diverged, but they spent just as much time together as always in the evenings... until Ellie met Luke and Sophie went away to university.

Now, in the hot French kitchen, surrounded by the smell of baking scones, the years melted away and it was just like old times. When the last batch went into the oven, Sophie made tea. Juliette had left about an hour before and the others weren't back, so it was just the two of them left.

"I've set a timer on my phone," Sophie said. "Let's go have our tea outside in the shade."

They sat on the grass, in the meagre shade from the trees.

"Thanks for doing all that work, Ells," Sophie said.

"I enjoyed it. It's been ages since we hung out together." It had been the most relaxing, if tiring, afternoon Ellie had had in a long time. She felt lighter for it, as though she'd put down a weight she hadn't known she was carrying. "And I'm glad I got to contribute to your wedding."

Sophie laughed. "You're contributing to my wedding, just by being here."

Ellie rolled her eyes. "I can't believe you're going to be a married woman soon."

Her friend made a face. "Don't say it like that. I'm just marrying the man I love. It's ... a nice thing." She leaned forward and patted Ellie's hand. "We'll still see each other though. I'll still be coming home to see Mum, so I'll see you then."

At the mention of home, the weight returned.

"What's the matter?" Sophie said. "Your face just dropped."

"Sorry. Just thinking about home and all the stuff I have to face when I get back. You know what dad and Luke are like."

"Luke is irrelevant now, right?"

Oh. Yes. So he was. "That's true," she said. "I'm still not used to it. You know, I've been half of Luke-and-Ellie for so long, it's like it was part of who I am."

"It's not," Sophie said, firmly. "You are so much more than 'half of Luke and Ellie.'" She shook her head.

"I know you didn't like him, but-"

"But what? I didn't like him. I tried, because you did, but no. He wasn't very nice, Ellie. Not even to you after a few years."

Ellie looked down at her tea and said nothing.

Sophie patted her hand again. "Look, love. I know it's hard when you've come out of a long term relationship. Why don't you chill out a bit? Flirt with one of our friends. Get off with someone. Have a holiday fling. Whatever. Because you can do that. You're single now."

Ellie started thoughtfully at the ground for a minute. "That's true," she murmured. "I am, aren't I?"

THAT EVENING, SHE SAT next to Ash and tried to keep focused. After a long day cooking, the wine went straight to her head and made her sleepy. She cupped her chin in her hands and listened to the conversation. The table had been cleared and the washing up done by the people who had not helped with the cooking. As there were more people now, it seemed to have taken no time at all.

It wasn't often she had nothing to do at home. Now that she was sitting still, she realised that at home, she was always rushing from one thing to another. Getting to work, getting home to put tea on for her and dad, getting ready for Luke. Always rushing. Nearly always late. Here, in this time, she had nothing to do. It was wonderful. She smiled to herself and leaned back to stretch out her arms. She overbalanced and nearly fell out of her chair. Ash caught her and steadied her, his arm around her waist. She leaned gratefully against him. He was so warm.

"Steady," he said, laughing. "How much have you had to drink, Ellie?"

"Not much," she said. "Not enough."

"Maybe a glass of water would be a good idea," he said. "To ward off the headache tomorrow." He made sure she was steady, and got up to fetch her a glass of water. She felt the absence of his arm around her. It was nice, being held. She wanted to be held again. What had Sophie said? A fling?

Ash returned with a glass of water, which he placed next to her wine glass. She noticed that he didn't insist she drank it, which struck her as nice. Luke wouldn't have done that. Come to think of it, Luke would have made her get her own water.

"Thank you," she said. "You are lovely."

He laughed and sat back down.

Helene said something and Ash turned to talk to her. Ellie rested her cheek in her hand and watched him. He was lovely. He was so kind. She liked kindness. It wasn't something she'd have automatically put at the top of desirable characteristics in a man, but it probably should have been. In the past, she had always put 'handsome' right at the top of the list, along with muscular. Luke had been handsome and muscular. Very much so. Was Ash?

She frowned, watching him in the pale glow of the LED lamps and fading sunset. He was browner than usual, with all the sun he was getting. His eyes and hair were so dark, it was almost unreal. He was handsome, in a nice guy kind of way. He moved an arm to make a point. He had nice forearms. Ellie smiled. She liked nice forearms.

He caught her eye. "What?" he said. There were little creases around his eyes when he smiled, like he did it a lot. She liked that too.

"Nothing." She shook her head and nearly lost her balance again.

"Woah." He moved closer. His arm was around her shoulder now. "Okay, I really think you should drink that water, Ellie."

"Hmpf. Bossy," she said. But she drank some water anyway. His arm was still around her shoulders. It was a nice, comforting thing. His arm was warm and solid. She laid her head against his shoulder. He gave her a surprised glance, but didn't object. His face was very close now and he smelled of sun cream. She slid sideways a little in her seat. His arm tightened around her. It really was nice to be held. Especially, she decided, to be held by Ash. Ellie sighed. The wine got the better of her and her eyes started to close of their own accord.

"I think maybe I should go to bed." Her eyelids felt impossibly heavy now.

He chuckled and she felt it vibrate through him. "Probably a good idea." There was no getting around it. She was attracted to him. She was sure there was a problem with that. Right now she couldn't remember what that could be.

"Come on." He hauled her to her feet. "Let's get you to your tent."

She linked her arm through his and leaned against him.

"You off to bed?" Sophie said, reaching up to pat Ellie's arm as they went past her.

"I am," said Ellie.

"I'll see this one to her tent and I'll come back," said Ash, firmly.

"Night night, bird," said Sophie. "I'll wake you up bright and early tomorrow."

Ellie leaned over and kissed the top of her friend's head. "Night, love."

They walked across the grass, Ellie staggering a little, so that she had to lean against Ash. Had to. "I haven't even drunk that much," she complained.

"No. I guess it's been a long day for you," said Ash. "I'm sorry I didn't stay and help."

"Oh no, it was fine. I got to be with Sophie. I miss her."

They reached the tent and Ash knelt down to unzip it for her. "In you go," he said.

Ellie yawned, suddenly almost too exhausted to stand. Somehow, it was important that she didn't crawl in head first. So undignified, with her arse sticking out of the tent. That would never do. She dropped down and scooched in backwards instead. "Ash," she said, peering out at his legs.

He hunkered down and his face appeared, eerie in the gloom. "Yes?"

"She was an idiot, you know that?"

"Who was?"

"That girl who dumped you. She's stupid. You're lovely."

Ash laughed softly. "Thank you, Ellie. I appreciate that. Now then, have you got everything you need?"

She yawned again. "I'm fine. G'night." She pulled herself the rest of the way in and found her sleeping back. "Night." She fumbled her way into it fully clothed and reached up to close the zip. Ash was still outside. For a second, she thought he was going to say something, but he seemed to change his mind. "Okay then. Good night," he said.

She zipped up the tent and promptly fell asleep.

Chapter 12

The morning of the wedding dawned bright and dewy. As promised, Sophie woke everyone up early by banging on a saucepan while Ethan shouted 'half an hour until breakfast' in several different languages.

Ellie sat up and stretched. "Ash?" she said, loudly enough for him to hear in the next tent. "You awake?"

"Hard not to be," Ash's voice grumbled through the walls of the tent. He yawned loudly. "How are you feeling this morning?"

"Not too terrible." Her mouth felt like it was coated in compost, but her head wasn't too bad. Thank goodness he'd made her drink water. "I'm going to make a dash for the bathroom to beat the rush."

But when she got to the house, someone was already in the bathroom. So she stepped outside to wait in the fresh air. The sun was still low and burning off a light mist. It glinted off dew at the end of leaves. With the scattering of tents at the far end of the lawn, it looked like something out of a seventies hippy movie. Ellie breathed in and felt the clarity of the air. Somewhere nearby there was coffee.

Her gaze drifted back towards her tent. As she watched, Ash crawled out of his tent. He stood up and stretched, making his t-shirt ride up and showing a few inches of toned, brown midriff. Used, as she was, to hanging out with thick set, sporty men, Ellie felt that there was something compact about Ash. It wasn't so much that he was smaller than most men she knew - he was about the same height as Luke, although he was thinner - It was almost as though he was packed more tightly into his body. Not for the first time, she wondered if that might be a good thing.

Someone came up to stand next to her. "Morning, bird," said Sophie. She thrust a mug towards her. "Coffee?"

"Oh, yes please!" Ellie took the mug. "Big day today," she said. "Nervous?"

Sophie beamed, her face more glorious than the sunlight. "Not really." She dipped her head and took a sip of coffee. "I'm marrying the man of my dreams. We're having a laid back sort of wedding, so there's nothing to be nervous about."

Ellie watched the softness of her friend's expression and couldn't help smiling back. "You're so lucky to have found someone who loves you as much and you love him."

"I've never been more sure of anything in my life, Ellie" said Sophie. She patted Ellie's arm. "There's someone out there for you too, you know. Now that Luke's not throwing his weight around, you might even have the chance to find him."

Ellie rolled her eyes. "Chance would be a fine thing."

Sophie glanced across the lawn towards the tents, where Ash had disappeared back into his, while the others were starting to wander towards the house. "What about Ash?" she said.

Ellie raised her mug to hide her face. "What about him?"

"He used to have a massive crush on you when we were at school."

Ellie took too big a mouthful of coffee and burned her mouth. "Ow."

"Yeah," Sophie continued. "He used to see you bring the bread into the shop and go all shy. Although, going all shy was pretty much Ash's MO back then. It's nice to see him come out of his shell."

"I had no idea," Ellie said. She'd barely noticed him when they were at school. The only reason she knew anything of him at all was because he was friends with Sophie and because she used to see him in the shop every weekend when, as Sophie had pointed out, she took the bread from the bakery to be sold in the shop. She'd seen him, but never noticed him. He was just some guy. Irrelevant.

Except now she knew him. She knew he was friendly and confident and stubborn. She knew he would put himself out to stop her from being in an uncomfortable position. She knew one side of his smile was higher than the other. She knew she could pick out his laugh out of a hundred voices.

"He's a good guy, you know," said Sophie knowingly. "You could do worse."

Ellie started to protest. "Oh no, there's nothing-" But Sophie had already wandered off.

EVERYONE HAD TO HELP prepare for the wedding. A lorry arrived with the marquee in it and the air was suddenly full of clanking and cheery shouts of the men constructing it.

Sophie and her Mother-in-law-to-be stood at the top of the trestle table with a large sheet, leaning over it like it was a battle plan. They divided everyone into teams. Decorations, set up, canapes. Ellie was on canapes. So was Ash.

"We're doing English puddings," Sophie told the small team. "Little scones with cream and jam, bread and butter pudding and Victoria sponges. My friend Ellie here is a baker, she will be coordinating you all." Sophie pointed to Ellie.

Ellie stepped up to the front. Three pairs of eyes turned to her and her face suddenly felt hot. "I ... um." She found Ash, who smiled at her. "I made most of the things earlier. We just need to put them together and decorate."

"I'll leave you to it," said Sophie. "If you need anything else, grab me or Ethan."

"We should be okay." Ellie looked at the covered trays in front of her. The bread and butter pudding had cooled overnight. Hopefully, the changes to the recipe that she'd made meant that it would hold firm when she cut it into squares. The Victoria sponges had been baked in small moulds, so putting them together would be relatively straightforward.

"Helene, can you help me with the bread and butter pudding?"

"Of course." Helene swiftly tied back her hair. "I shall wash my hands again and be right back." That left Ash and Tomas. "Okay," Ellie said. "I need someone to cut the scones in half. It's a little fiddly."

"Fiddly?" said Tomas.

"Tricky," said Ash. "Difficult."

"Ah."

Ellie realised she needed to slow down a little. She cut one of the scones in half. "We put the cream into the piping bag," she picked up a bag and swiftly filled it. "Twist and pipe a swirl." She demonstrated with practiced ease. "And a dollop of jam on top."

"How do you stop the jam from just … sliding off?" asked Tomas.

"You see how I've left a small gap in the middle of the swirl."

"I thought you had to do jam first," said Ash.

Ellie glared at him. "We're not in Cornwall."

"No. No. Sorry miss." He grinned at her, apparently unfazed.

"Just for that," she said. "You get to be on scone slicing duty. Those things took me ages to make. Don't ruin them." She held the knife by the blade and shook the handle at him.

"I promise, I will be as careful as humanly possible." He took the knife.

"Tomas, can you do the jam, please?"

He nodded and moved across the stand next to Ash. Helene returned, carrying three large trays. "Juliette says we should use these."

Helene put the trays down to reveal that they had already been lined with paper doilies.

"Lovely." Ellie pointed to a stack of mini cake cases. "We put each pudding on one of these. We'll put alternating lines of each pudding down on the tray and people can pick what they want."

They stood side by side, working together. Helene cut the tray bake into neat squares and they lined them up on the tray. Ellie carefully assembled the Victoria sponges and sprinkled icing sugar over each one before placing it on the tray. As the boys finished the scones, they too were placed in neat rows.

At another table, people were making finger sandwiches. Someone found portable speakers and put some Abba on.

Soon most people were singing along, moving to the music as they worked. Ellie felt a strange sense of companionship; that sense of being part of something bigger. It was a feeling she hadn't had since she'd stopped playing Netball. She found that she was smiling as she sang along.

Every so often, she sneaked a glance at Ash. He and Tomas had an efficient system going where Ash piped the cream on and Tomas spooned on the jam. Ash was concentrating so hard, the tip of his tongue stuck out of the corner of his mouth. It was adorable. He finished the row he was working on and caught her looking at him. He smiled. She felt something connect, deep inside. There was no getting away from it. She fancied him.

Ellie forced herself to concentrate on the task at hand. She had a job to do here.

Assembling the Victoria sponges took longer than she expected, because they had to take such care to make sure the cake didn't disintegrate. As the morning wore on, Ellie was aware of the air getting warmer. They needed these to be done and taken back into the house soon. She carefully placed the last Victoria sponge into place and surveyed the trays. A few more scones and they were done.

"Nice work, everyone," she said.

The others grinned at her.

"Boss," said Ash. "We had a few … accidents." He pointed to a couple of scones that had crumbled at the edges. "What do we do with those?"

She had only two disintegrated slices of Victoria sponge and Helene had managed to plate up all the squares of bread and butter pudding with no mishaps whatsoever. Ellie rolled her eyes in mock horror. "Well, if Sophie has enough for her canapes, I guess we'll just have to eat them."

"Yes!" Tomas punched the air. "Just let us finish these last few."

He placed the last scones in place. Ellie and Helene carefully stretched cling wrap over the trays. They picked up a tray each and carried it into the house.

After the bright sunlight, the house looked very dark and the cool air was a relief.

Helene popped her head in the door and asked a question in French. Ellie once again wished she'd paid more attention at school.

"She says to put them through here. Come." Helene led her into one of the rooms that was off the hallway.

They were in a living room. Or, it would have been a living room on a normal day. Today the furniture had been pushed to one side, for some reason, so that they were under the windows. Trestle tables took up the middle of the room. Helene found a space on the table and they put their trays down next to a tray of cling wrapped finger sandwiches. Music and laughter filtered in through the windows.

Ellie looked around, realising it was the first time she'd really had a chance to see inside the room. It still felt dark compared to outside. The shutters had been thrown open so that sunlight poured in to make bright patches on the floor. She realised that the furniture was below the windows because someone had taken care to put the tables out of the light. Clever.

Helene surveyed the trays of canapes. "That," she said. "Looks very good. Professional, even." She turned to Ellie. "You are very good."

The approval in her voice seemed genuine and Ellie felt a little kick of pride. "Thanks." The idea that someone as clever and intimidating as Helene would be impressed by her baking skills seemed ridiculous and brilliant at the same time.

"So," said Helene. "Shall we get back and see what else we can help with?"

Ellie smiled back at her. "Sure. Come on."

They got back out into the sunshine to find that Tomas and Ash had been recruited to put up bunting. Soon Ellie was standing with her arms full of bunting while Ash went up a ladder, which Tomas was holding steady, to tie bunting onto a tree. The Abba album was playing round again and everyone was singing along to Super Trouper. Ellie joined in and felt happier than she had done in the longest time.

"Done," said Ash. He came down the ladder. "That one next?"

They moved, in a group, over to the next tree, Ellie playing out the line of bunting as she went. She stood a little distance away and watched the boys find a stable spot. As Ash went up the ladder, she caught herself idly watching the way the muscles corded in his arms as he pulled himself up the rungs. Why had she ever thought of him as skinny? Toned. That was probably the word she needed. Was all of him that toned? What did those arms feel like?

Ahead of her, Ash paused part way up and reached out an arm. His eyes met hers.

For a second, she froze. Had he been able to read her thoughts? Oh god, how embarrassing!

"Ellie?" said Ash. His gaze moved to the bunting she had forgotten she was holding.

The spell shattered. "Oh," she said. "Bunting. Sorry." She stepped forward and handed it up to him, standing on her tiptoes to pass him the line. "Sorry," she said again.

He paused for a fraction of a second, a tiny frown on his face. He raised an eyebrow as though to ask her if she was okay. She smiled. The frown cleared and he carried on up.

Ellie relaxed. She shifted the loop of bunting from one arm to the other and thought about what Sophie had said that morning. Ash was nice. Kind. And ... she sneaked a glance upwards, where he was stretching out to the side to loop the bunting on a second branch, his t-shirt stretching out over a taut back ... and attractive. He wasn't the sort that she went normally for, but she could get used to the way he cared. And the way he didn't question her choices. And the way he listened.

He clattered down again. "How many more can we get to, d'you think?" he asked.

Tomas looked at the loop in Ellie's arm. "There's about another twelve meters, I estimate," he said. "We can perhaps do one more."

Ellie nodded. They set off to do the next tree.

Chapter 13

It seemed very strange to be getting ready for a wedding sitting cross legged in a tent. Ellie carefully twisted her hair and pinned it up, wishing she had a bigger mirror than the one on the top of her washbag. She could have tried the bathroom in the house, but there was bound to be a queue. On the other hand, she couldn't see much in here. Grabbing her makeup, she crawled out of the tent, careful not to kneel on her dress. Luckily, it was dry.

In the sunshine, she brushed down her dress to check it wasn't wrinkled. It wasn't terribly fancy. It was a simple cotton dress with tiny blue flowers on it. She had a matching blue ribbon to go on her sun hat. Together the combination was cool, but elegant. Perfect for a summer wedding.

Across the way from her, Tomas was standing, shirtless, talking animatedly to one of the other guys. He spotted Ellie looking at him and gave her a cheeky wink. She shook her head and turned away. Ash was standing a little way behind his tent, crouching slightly. He appeared to be combing his hair. She walked round to where he was. He had hung his mirror, slightly larger than hers, on a branch of a nearby tree.

"Oh hey," she said. "Can I borrow your mirror for a minute?"

"Just a second." He carefully ran the comb over his hair. He was wearing a suit, with a cream shirt and no tie. He must have shaved, because the stubble he'd been sporting over the last few days had disappeared. Without the stubble, he looked tidier. The lines of his face were more defined. He had excellent bone structure. He had got even browner than before. This too made him look more taut than he had before. Concentrating on his hair, he had pressed his lips together. They were nice lips. Dark pink edged with brown. They looked … warm.

She was staring again. She had to stop doing that. And she still hadn't done her makeup. "Oh come on," she said. "Budge up. You look great."

She nudged him with her shoulder and he looked down at her. He was so close that she could smell his aftershave. She remembered his arm around her the night before. They had been this close then too. His gaze met hers and a wave of heat washed over her. "S … sorry," she murmured.

"It's okay," he said, softly, and stepped away.

She wanted to follow him, but after making such a fuss about the mirror, she had to use it. She did her makeup, trying to focus, but his presence seemed to set something prickling between her shoulder blades. She gave herself a last check in the mirror. She had gone for an understated look. Light eyeshadow, a hint of blush and lipgloss.

"How do I look?" she turned.

His expression said it all. Ellie suddenly felt like she was the most beautiful woman in the garden. She smiled. Ash cleared his throat. "You look amazing," he said, with such sincerity that she felt that warmth all over again.

He reached towards her, and for a moment, she thought he was going to take her hand, but he was merely taking the mirror down. Once it was safely stashed away and Ash had zipped up both their tents, so that she didn't have to kneel on the ground and mess up her dress, he gave her his arm and they headed down to the house.

THE BRIDE WORE YELLOW. It wasn't traditional, but it was the most joyous thing that Ellie had ever seen. Sophie glowed, radiant in her happiness. Ethan glowed too. A bubble seemed to have formed around them.

The ceremony was held in the local town hall, in a formal room with huge windows, where everyone stood beaming, while the bride and groom said their vows, first in French and then in English. Ellie stood behind Sophie's parents as part of the small 'bride's family party' and watched, a lump in her throat. Sophie's mum was in tears and her dad looked like he was not far off tears himself. They were so happy for her, Ellie felt emotional just seeing the pride on their faces.

Oh, she was going to cry. She always cried at weddings. She hastily looked in the small handbag and realised she'd forgotten to grab a tissue. How embarrassing. Ash nudged her and pressed a napkin into her hand. She glanced over her shoulder to say thank you and thought his eyes looked damp too. She smiled as she turned around, dabbing her eyes. Luke used to tease her for crying at weddings and at the cinema. Ash, it seemed, wouldn't be able to do that because he was a big softie too.

They were given rose petals to throw at the happy couple. Afterwards, they all crammed into cars and were taken back to the house where the caterers had arrived and the marquee was buzzing.

Ellie picked up a glass of champagne. Ash appeared beside her. He snagged a couple of snacks from one of the waiters who went past. "They turned out nice," he said. He was holding two mini scones that they'd made earlier. "Everyone here is eating stuff we made," he said, with a goofy smile. "I like that. We're an integral part of Sophie's wedding, rather than just guests."

"I like that too." She caught sight of Sophie, a radiant figure in yellow, and felt her eyes moisten again. Sophie was her best friend. She was glad she'd been able to have a part in her wedding, no matter how small. When Sophie had first said she wanted to study French and business, Luke had laughed at her and asked her what she expected to find in France that she couldn't get in England. At the time, Ellie had secretly agreed with him, but now, seeing the way her friend looked up at her new husband, she knew the answer. Ethan. That's what Sophie had found in France that she couldn't find at home. This specific man, who was perfect for her.

Ellie's smile dropped. What if there was someone out there for her ... and he wasn't in England? How would she ever find him? How would she even begin?

Helene, her arm threaded through that of one of the other guys, walked past, laughing. She raised her glass towards Ellie and Ellie waved back. She couldn't believe she'd found Helene intimidating when she'd got here. It had only been four days! So much had changed.

Coming to Sophie's wedding had been an eye-opening experience, completely different to anything she'd done before. She looked around at the marquee, where ribbons she had helped curl and balloons she had helped blow up stirred in the warm breeze. Outside, across the sun soaked grass, voices chattered in different languages, punctuated by laughter. She was surprised to be able to catch a few phrases of French here and there. After four days of being surrounded by it, a lot of her GCSE French was coming back to her. She must have learned more than she'd thought, which was a nice thing to find out.

"You okay, Ellie?" Ash's voice was soft. "Lost you for a minute there."

"I'm fine." She looked up at him and smiled.

His expression twitched, and his lips moved a little without forming words, as though he'd forgotten what he'd been going to say. "You look happy," he said at last.

"I am," she said. "I was just thinking I'm glad I came."

His eyes darkened. "I'm glad you came too."

Ellie couldn't take her eyes off his. The light brown of his irises, the widened pupils, the intensity of his expression. Her attention moved to his mouth. Those lips she had admired a few hours ago were close now. If she leaned in, just a little closer, she could kiss him. Right now, without a doubt, she wanted to.

Someone walked past, jolting her arm. She spun around to look at them. They apologised in French. Ellie said 'it's nothing', also in French, much to her own surprise. When she turned back, Ash had moved. The moment was gone. The disappointment she felt was crushing.

"Um, we should probably go sit down," he said. "That's what I was coming to tell you. I've saved you a seat at the same table as Tomas and Helene and the rest of them."

"Oh," she said. "Yes. That would be lovely. Cheers."

He turned to lead the way and casually held out his hand. Heart galloping, Ellie took it.

APPARENTLY, SONGS AND sketches were a thing that happened in European weddings. Since most of it was in rapid-fire French, Ellie didn't fully understand the words, but there were enough physical cues and gags for her to follow what was going on.

Later, the band played folk tunes and the first dance ended with Sophie and Ethan grabbing the hands of a new partner each and dragging them onto the dancefloor. The numbers multiplied and Ellie suddenly found herself being spun around the dancefloor by Tomas. She laughed, whirling around and trying to keep up with the steps. The caller was giving instructions, but she couldn't understand them, so she had to take her cue from the other people around her. The dance finished, and she hurried to the side of the dancefloor before the next one started. She grabbed a drink.

Ash came up and snagged a drink too. He grinned at her. He had shed his suit jacket and his shirt was open at the collar. The hair that he'd so carefully combed was sticking up in all directions. It all had the effect of making Ellie's urge to kiss him even stronger.

His eyes shone. "I haven't done that sort of dancing since school. Do you remember?"

At school, in the last two weeks before Christmas, the PE lessons were given over to Ceilidh dances. The band talked them through the steps and they burned up their energy dancing. She had forgotten all about those.

The band started up again. "I'm going to sit this one out," said Ellie.

Ash shrugged. "Me too." He put his drink down. "I'm boiling." He unbuttoned the cuffs on his shirt and rolled up his sleeves, revealing those taut forearms. Ellie could barely tear her eyes away. Ash picked up his drink again and leaned against the table behind him. She didn't know where to look. Everywhere her gaze settled, she could just lick him.

Ellie turned fully to watch the dancing and, oh, so casually, leaned back against him. When Ash didn't object, she relaxed. His body moved slightly against hers and he swayed to the music. His breath stirred the hairs on the back of her neck. The warmth of him enveloped her and the need to be closer, to have more of him, increased.

Ash took a sip of his drink. To do this, he had to lean forward, press closer to her. She glanced over her shoulder and saw the movement of his throat as he swallowed. Oh my. He brought his hand down, still holding his glass in his fingertips, and rested his wrist against her hip. Ellie could barely breathe for lust now. She put her own drink down and reached across her body to wrap her fingers around his wrist. "Shall we go ... somewhere else?"

He didn't reply, but the intensity of his expression told her everything she needed to know. Hand in hand, they left the marquee and the dancing. Outside, the sun was setting and the evening was cooling. There were people everywhere. There was no privacy to be had.

"Tent?" said Ash.

Ellie nodded and marched across the grass. "Mine's bigger." She dropped to her knees, not caring about the dress. She unzipped the tent, turned around and scooched in backwards, so that she could kick her shoes off before she pulled her legs in. Ash appeared next to her, leaning out of the tent to take his shoes off. She ran her hand down his back, feeling the muscle underneath the shirt that was stretched over it. Ash gave the smallest moan. Finally kicking his shoes off he pulled himself into the tent.

And then his mouth was on hers. Her fingers were in his thick hair. His kiss was gentle and somehow intense. She pressed herself closer, wanting more. Except ... she drew back. "I don't have any condoms," she said, suddenly. She hadn't expected to need them.

Ash's chuckle was deep and resonated at the base of her throat. "Don't worry." He pressed a kiss on her neck. "We can work around that."

He shifted position so that she could curl closer to his lean body. She hooked her leg over his hip and felt his hard thigh press between hers in response. She felt like she was on fire, glowing on the inside. His lips whispered against her throat, sending little bolts of pleasure down her spine.

His hand slid, slowly and deliberately up the back of her leg and she shivered with every inch. In the darkening cocoon of the tent, Ellie gave herself up to the sensations and let him tease her until she came apart completely.

Afterwards, she lay snuggled up next to him, relaxed and sated. Next to her, she felt Ash's breathing slow down and the weight of his arm, draped around her waist, increase as he drifted off to sleep. Clearly Ash's university years had provided him with quite an education. He was a kind and thoughtful lover and she felt ... treasured. She sighed and closed her eyes.

It had never been like this with Luke.

The thought was like an ice cold bucket of water. Her eyes flew open. Why was she thinking of Luke? Now of all times. She tensed. Ash stirred.

Ellie lay very still, her mind racing. Tomorrow, they were going home. Away from the sunshine and the sun warmed peaches. Back home, to where her Dad was probably still furious with her and Luke was still her freshly shed ex. She shifted position, so that she could look over her shoulder at the shape of Ash behind her. What would happen with Ash? She couldn't imagine going home with him as her boyfriend. She was only just getting over not being half of Luke and Ellie. Of course, everyone would get used to it ... eventually. But try as she might, she couldn't picture it. She had been with Luke for so long, everything at home was tainted with him.

As for Ash ... at home Ash was the quiet, bookish kid behind the counter at the cornershop. She stroked the arm that was draped across her. Except he wasn't that now, was he? He was almost a different person altogether. A man who laughed when he fell in the river and stuck his tongue out of the corner of his mouth when he concentrated on piping thickened cream onto scones. A man who made her feel like the most beautiful woman in the room. She could be happy with him.

So why was she feeling guilty? Was it a race thing? She thought back over her last week and the friendships she'd had over the years. No. It wasn't that. Something else. The answer came to her, blindingly obvious. She still thought of herself as Luke's girl, even though she wasn't anymore. She liked Ash, but she couldn't have any sort of future with him, because a small part of her still belonged to Luke.

She gently moved Ash's arm out of her way and sat up. He startled and she knew she'd woken him.

"Ellie?" he murmured, his voice still thick from sleep. "Is something wrong?"

And now she'd ruined the moment. Tears filled her eyes. She sniffed and wiped them away.

Ash sat up. "Did I hurt you somehow?" he said, his voice was quicker now. "I didn't mean to."

She shook her head. "You didn't hurt me. You ... you were wonderful." It was too dark to see his expression properly, but she could tell she had upset him. It was only natural. "It's not you. It's me." She hugged her knees. "I'm so ..."

"So?" He pulled his own knees up, increasing the space between them. She could barely make out his face in shadows, but she knew she was hurting him. He thought he'd done something wrong, when all he'd done was show her what she'd been missing out on. If she told him what had gone wrong ... he would be so hurt. He had made stars explode for her and then, the first thing she'd thought of when she could think again was her ex. What did that say about her? Tears welled and spilled over. She sniffed and wiped them away again.

"Oh. Oh, Ellie, don't cry." His voice was full of confusion. "Whatever it was that I did. I'm sorry."

"You didn't do anything. It's me. I'm such a cow." She broke down completely. The sobs shook her whole body.

He touched her hesitantly, as though asking for permission. When she leaned into him, he put his arms around her. "What's wrong?"

She couldn't tell him. That would be a terrible thing to do to him.

"Ellie, you're scaring me now."

But she had to tell him, otherwise he would blame himself. "I'm so sorry," she said, wiping tears off her face. "I don't think I'm over my ex."

He didn't move, but his arms tensed. "Oh." For a moment there was no sound, but their breathing. "So just now ... you were thinking of him when ..." There was no warmth in his voice now.

"Oh no, no," she said. "It's just after-"

He removed his arms from around her and moved back. "Cheers."

"Not like that, Ash. I didn't mean to hurt you. I feel bad. Like I'm cheating on him. And that's not right."

He started to crawl out of the tent, not bothering to try and locate his shirt.

"Ash, wait. I-"

"What, Ellie? You've just told me that I'm not as good as your ex and you expect me to stay?" The bitterness in his voice cut through her. She felt terrible, but he was right. He couldn't stay. Not now.

She listened to him pull his shoes back on and walk away. The sound of him unzipping his tent was loud in the now quiet night.

What was wrong with her? She hugged her knees and cried as quietly as she could.

Chapter 14

S he was woken up by the sound of voices coming from a distance. Sophie and Ethan were setting off for their honeymoon early that morning. Ellie sat up. By the light of her phone, she found a jumper and pulled it on over her dress. Pulling on her trainers, she let herself out of the tent. It was barely light. The sky was dark blue, rather than black, but dawn hadn't fully broken yet. Ash's tent was zipped up.

Quietly, she walked across the dewy grass towards the house, where the lights were on. The back door wasn't locked. She let herself in and went to the hall where Sophie was checking her handbag while Ethan lined up their bags.

"Ellie," said Sophie.

"I came to say goodbye," Ellie said.

Sophie gave her a hug. "Bye bird. I'll see you in a few months when we come over for Christmas, yeah?"

"I'll look forward to that." Ellie squeezed her back. "Have the best time on honeymoon."

"Of course I will!" Sophie rested her cheek against Ellie's. "You and Ash, huh? I saw you guys sneaking off. I'm so happy for you! He's such a lovely guy. You two make an adorable couple."

Ellie willed her face not to give her away. Sophie was going on her honeymoon. She didn't need to know what a pile of crap

Ellie had made of things. "Yeah," she said. "He is amazing." She meant it. He was. It was her that was the problem.

Sophie released her. A few other members of the family appeared, most of them in night clothes. Ellie watched the flurry of goodbyes. As they all stood on the steps to wave goodbye, Ellie went back outside again.

The dawn was in evidence now and the birds were singing. Ellie took in the, now familiar, sight and realised that this was the last morning that she would stand here and admire the view. That afternoon she was going home. With Ash. It was going to be so awkward.

A zip opened and Helene appeared, not from her own tent, but from one of the new ones belonging to someone who had been there just for the wedding night. She was still in her wedding clothes and had her shoes in her hand. Spotting Ellie, she gave her a little wave and carried on with her walk of shame back to her own tent.

Ellie waved back. Her gaze drifted towards Ash's tent, still silent, next to hers. She had ruined a perfectly good friendship by still being in love with her ex. It would have been better if she'd acknowledged that she had a bit of a crush on Ash and then left it at that. But no. She had to go and ruin everything properly.

She made her way back to her tent. Inside, she found Ash's shirt. She put her face to it and breathed in the smell of him. Oh Ash. Carefully, she folded it. She would return it as soon as she heard him stir.

As quietly as she possibly could, she packed up her things. By the time she heard other voices, she was sitting, fully dressed in her tent, with all her belongings packed and almost ready to go.

She came out to see that the long tables were being set out again. Normally, she would have gone and got Ash, but she couldn't today, so she grabbed her wash bag and went out by herself. Eventually, she ended up in the kitchen, helping Juliette make huge cafetieres of coffee and warm up the pastries that had arrived from the bakery. They worked together, communicating without having a language in common. Occasionally, a relative would pop in and there would be a conversation that Ellie couldn't fully follow, but she knew they were talking about breakfast or, more likely, checking that Sophie and Ethan had got off on time. It was hard to believe that just a week ago, she had felt awkward in the presence of people whose language she didn't understand. Now she knew that they had better things to do than to talk about her. Just as Ash had tried to tell her on that first night.

She still hadn't seen him. Part of her was dreading it. Part of her just wanted to get it over with.

By the time she finally carried a big tray of croissants out to the table, a lot of hungover people were sitting around the table, but her eyes went straight to Ash. He was sitting with Tomas, cradling a mug of coffee. He spotted her and looked away. Ellie supposed she deserved that, but it still stung. Well, she may as well tackle this head on.

She grabbed a chair and carried it over. "Mind if I join you?"

Without waiting for him to answer, she plonked the chair down. Ash reluctantly shifted along a bit. Ellie grabbed a croissant and some coffee and sat down.

"Ash -" she said.

"I was just saying to Tomas," Ash said, not looking at her. "That our train is at lunchtime. We won't get home until really late. Well, to London, anyway. You've got a bit of a way to go after that."

Tomas's eyes flicked from one to the other. "I can give you a lift to the station. I am staying until tomorrow, then driving back to the Netherlands."

"Oh, that would be very kind," Ash said. He was speaking quickly, as though afraid Ellie might get a word in.

"Yes," said Ellie. "That is very nice of you. Thank you."

Tomas raised his mug. "My pleasure."

Helene, who had been sitting with one of Ethan's cousins, came over. She passed a piece of paper over to Ellie. "I will be going soon," she said. "I wanted to say to keep in touch. Here is my email address."

"Oh thank you," said Ellie. "I should give you mine."

"I have your insta. I can contact you that way. Or you email me, when you get home."

Ellie stood up and stepped away from the table, so that she could give Helene a hug. She was genuinely sad to say goodbye. It was hard to believe that she had thought this woman aloof and intimidating at one time. "It was lovely to meet you," she said, and meant it.

"You too Ellie. I will miss your baking."

"If you're ever in Yorkshire, come by the bakery. My boss makes the most amazing cinnamon buns."

"I hope things go well with Ash," said Helene, with a sly smile.

"Um, no. That's ... no."

"Oh, but I thought last night-"

Ellie shook her head. "No. It didn't work out."

"No?" Helene's eyebrows shot up. "That is a shame. Well, keep trying. I am sure he is interested."

"Right. Yes. Thanks." She stepped away quickly, before Helene tried to pry for details.

After breakfast, she asked Ash if he wanted any help dismantling his tent. For a second he looked like he was going to refuse, but he glared at his tent and nodded. "Thanks."

"Ash," said Ellie. "Can we talk about this?"

Finally, he looked up at her. "What is there to talk about, Ellie. We hooked up. You changed your mind. You're allowed."

"But I've hurt you," she said. "I hate that. You're important to me. I don't want to lose you as a friend."

Ash closed his eyes and sighed. "Ellie." He opened his eyes again, his expression pained. "I've liked you, at some level, since we were at school. We've been friends, even though I wanted more and after last night ... I'm not sure I can handle going back to being friends again. Not yet. I'm sorry."

She stared at him, feeling like she'd lost something precious. "I'm so sorry."

"Yeah," he said. "Me too." Another sigh. "So, about this tent..."

"Oh yes. Right."

They got the tents packed up, with quiet efficiency, working together with minimal chat. Before long, all that remained was two big backpacks and two flattened patches of grass.

AS THE EUROSTAR DREW out of Paris and sped towards home, Ellie felt a weight increasing in her limbs. Her dad still hadn't been in touch, even though she had texted him every day. She had also texted her aunt Jane, who had texted back four words 'I'm looking after him', which was as much a telling off as a note of reassurance.

She chewed on her lip and wondered what sort of a reception she could expect when she got home. Nothing nice, probably.

She glanced across at Ash, who was slumped in his seat, apparently completely absorbed in his reading. Ordinarily, she would have talked to him and he would have made her feel better even for a short while, but since they'd left the village, he had been distant. Oh, he was still polite and kind, helping her with her bags and making sure she was okay, but there was no warmth in it anymore. The stopover in Paris, which had been such an eye opener on the way down, had been a sterile affair. They had sat opposite each other, bags awkwardly rammed around their legs. Ellie had ordered the coffees, which made her feel like she'd come a long way. Ash had complimented her on it, but there was no smile. No teasing twinkle in his eyes.

Ellie sighed and rested her head against the glass window. She missed him. They had become really close during their holiday and she'd messed it all up by giving into a mad impulse of lust.

He flicked a page with a finger and she had a sudden image of those fingers doing other things. Her face flared at the thought and she turned away. Did she really regret it? It had been wonderful while it was happening. But there was that awful feeling of guilt afterwards. She'd felt like she was cheating on Luke. She had missed Luke too. And if she was still thinking about Luke, it wasn't right to string Ash along. He deserved better than that.

Ugh. She squeezed her eyes shut. Why did it all have to be so complicated?

IT WAS LATE BY THE time Ellie got home. She quietly let herself into the house. Her dad's coat was hanging up and the TV was on in the living room.

"Dad?" she put her head round the door.

He turned his head. "Oh, you're back are ye?" He looked back at the telly.

Okay. So that was how it was going to be. Oh well, she wasn't sure why she'd expected him to be any different. She turned the lights on and went to the kitchen, bracing herself to the state it might be in.

To her surprise, it looked entirely normal. The washing up was on the draining board, drying. She had only been away a week. How much mess did she think he'd make? Perhaps Aunt Jane had cleaned up when she came.

Having put the kettle on, she peeked in the fridge. There was a Tupperware container with what looked like pasta in it. Milk, cheese, bacon, the usual stuff. She closed the fridge and stared at the kettle as it started to boil. Somehow, she had expected her absence to have some effect. She looked after her dad, cooked for him and generally kept an eye on the house, because she felt it was her job. But maybe she didn't need to. Maybe he was fine all on his own.

The kettle boiled. She went back to the living room.

"Do you want a cuppa dad?"

He didn't say anything. The atmosphere in the room was stiff with tension. Ellie sighed. Fine. She withdrew.

"I'll have tea, if you're making," he said, without turning round.

"Okay." He was talking to her. It was progress.

She made two teas, grabbed a biscuit each, and took it through to him. "Here you go, Dad."

He grunted. "Ta."

Back in the kitchen, she sat at the kitchen table and took out her phone. There weren't many messages for her. She texted Aunt Jane to say she was back. A whole load of notifications had appeared on her Instagram feed since she'd uploaded the pictures while on the long journey up from London. She looked through.

She scrolled through pictures of her in her nice dress, smiling. There were photos from most days, she went through them backwards, the holiday unwinding from selfies of her and the bride, to slightly blurry ones taken in the evening before, to bright sunny ones. She hadn't taken any pictures of Ash, but there were hints of him in almost every picture. A brown arm or shoulder, just at the edge of a shot, a figure in the background. And, on at least one occasion, it was he who had taken the photo. Each time she spotted him, she felt another stab of sadness. She missed him.

She turned the phone face down and looked around her. After the memories of France, this kitchen with its beige and green walls and peeling Formica cupboard doors looked shabby and old. She was so used to it, she'd stopped noticing that it needed work. The wallpaper was loose in one corner and the window frames could do with a lick of paint. Luke had helped her dad redo the floor a few years back, so at least the lino was relatively new. But everything else looked terribly neglected. Ellie sighed.

Footsteps made her jump. She turned her head to watch her father walk in. He looked no different. She had only been away for less than a week, even if it felt like much longer.

He stood by the door and studied her. "You've got a tan," he said.

She couldn't tell if he disapproved or not. "Yeah. It was lovely and sunny."

"Hmph." He took his mug to the sink. "You had a good time, did ye?"

"I did, thanks."

"And the wedding? How was it?"

She had sent him several texts that day, of course he hadn't replied to any of them. "It was beautiful. Sophie was so happy."

"Mmm." He turned around and looked at her, his head to one side. His gaze moved over her face as though he were checking her for defects.

"I have some photos if you want to see." She turned her phone back up and found her photo folder.

"I saw them," he said.

Ellie frowned. "You did?"

"I saw your Luke in the pub. He showed me your Insta-whatsit page. You looked like you were having a good time."

There was so much to unpack in that sentence. First of all, he wasn't her Luke. She didn't know how she felt about her dad being able to see her Instagram page. She tried to think what she'd said on it. She had been fairly careful not to get any people on it, apart from Sophie and Ethan on their wedding day. She had definitely taken care to leave Ash out of any photos. She didn't want to think about her reasons for doing that.

"You had a good time, then," Dad said, again, as though he was trying to reassure himself that it was possible.

"I did, Dad. I'm sorry I was angry when I left, but I'm really glad I went. I got to spend time with Sophie and I made little puddings for her wedding and it was all ..." She spread out her hands. "All such a great experience."

"I suppose you'll be wanting to go abroad again soon, now you've got the taste for it," he said. He was looking at a spot on the table now.

She realised that this was the crux of what was bothering him. "I don't know, Dad. I'm not in any rush right this minute, but it's not so bad, you know." She softened her voice. "I came back, didn't I?"

He said nothing, but he darted a quick glance at her.

"I missed you, Dad," she said. Genuinely, she had. Perhaps not as much as he'd hoped she would, but she had missed him.

Now he looked up, his expression less severe than a minute ago. "I'm glad you're back." With that, he nodded and disappeared back down to the living room. Ellie stared after him and smiled. For Dad, that was practically a declaration of love.

LYING IN HER BED, ELLIE scrolled through her photos again and tried not to think about why she'd been so careful to leave Ash out of them. She wasn't ashamed of her connection to him. She just didn't want Luke to see it. With a sigh, she lowered the phone onto her chest. Her dad's assumption that they were back together - she had definitely told him she'd split up with Luke, so the only way he'd think they were together is if Luke had told him otherwise. Why would he do that?

She picked up her phone again and scrolled past the pictures from France, back to a selfie of her and Luke together. How did she feel about him? She felt he still had enough claim on her for her to feel guilty about Ash. Why was that? Did she still love him at some level? She had been happy with him once.

It was all so confusing. She had no idea how she felt about Luke anymore. And until she worked that out, she would always feel bad about seeing anyone else. Ellie sighed. She was going to have to see Luke again at some point. She would know when she saw him how she felt. If she felt scared or annoyed ... then that should be telling enough. Hopefully.

Turning her phone off, she plugged it into charge and turned her bedroom light off. Her love life might be a muddle at the moment, but at least she and dad were okay now. Maybe everything else would look better in the morning.

Chapter 15

It was weird getting up the next morning and getting ready for work. She got downstairs, just as her father was heading out. "Will you be in later, Dad?" She asked his retreating back.

He paused in the act of pulling on his coat. "Er … not for tea, no."

That was odd. "Have you got something on?" she said, trying to remember what day of the week it was. Not pub quiz night.

He shrugged on his coat. "I'm going to the pub," he said. He wouldn't meet her eyes. Her senses prickled.

"Oh aye? Is something on at the pub?"

"No, not as such. Just going for a drink." He sidled towards the door, as though anxious to get going. "I'll see you when I get home. Don't wait up."

"Sure..." Ellie took a sip of her coffee. Strange. It wasn't so much that he was going to the pub on the wrong night. It was, after all, an odd time. She had gone away without him to a foreign country for the first time. She had expected more anger from him, which hadn't materialised. And now this. Very odd.

She glanced at the clock. Better get a move on.

SUE GREETED HER LIKE a returning hero. "How was it?" she demanded before Ellie had even taken her coat off.

"It was wonderful. I made these amuse bouche for Sophie's wedding and they looked so sweet." There was so much to tell Sue that the words came out in a tumble.

Sue laughed. "Okay, tell you what. Let's get today's displays done and then, if we have a minute, you can tell me all about it."

Ellie nodded, put on her apron, tied back her hair and washed her hands. Before long, she was setting out cakes and helping Sue with the cream buns, as though she'd never been away. As she worked, she talked. The more she told Sue about her holiday, the more she realised how much it had changed her. She had started it frightened and suspicious, half expecting it to be a horrible experience that she was only putting up with because her best friend had invited her to her wedding. But now, she had friends who were from other countries. Last month, she barely had friends who weren't from Yorkshire.

It was difficult not to mention Ash. Without him, she would have just hidden in the kitchens on the pretext of helping Ethan's mum and never gone out to meet people. He had pushed and pulled her to join in. He had dug into her prejudices and given her the confidence to see beyond them. She was a better person for knowing him.

"I'm glad you had a good time," said Sue, smiling. "I knew it would do you good. You seem to have come out of your shell a bit."

Ellie laughed. "I didn't know I was in a shell."

"You were, love. You just couldn't see it." Sue paused and looked as though she was having an internal battle. "I think

..." she said, cautiously. "I think it probably did your dad some good too."

"Oh?"

"He needed a bit of time to remember who he was too." Sue put a two layer rectangular cake on a stand and got the icing kit out. "He put everything on hold to look after you when your mum left. I think it was good for him to remember that he's more than just your dad."

Ellie opened her mouth to comment, then closed it again. Was that true? Maybe it was. She hadn't thought of her dad like that, but yes, he had always been there for her, whether she wanted him to be or not.

Her stomach growled. She looked up at the clock. It was late morning. She should probably take her lunch now, before the lunchtime crowd showed up. "Can I take lunch early?"

"So long as you're back before the rush." Sue was bending over the drawings she'd made for the cake. Judging by the asymmetrical shape of it, it was one of the bespoke cakes.

"What's that one going to be?" Ellie hung up her apron and went to the fridge to get her sandwich.

"Fortieth birthday cake with a Harry Potter theme."

Ellie eyed the two stacked rectangles. "Trunks packed to take to Hogwarts?" Sue had done that cake before. It always went down a treat.

"Yes. This one should be straightforward. Mrs Howard wants a stegosaurus cake for her nephew. I was going to do the generic dinosaur, but my mould is T-Rex and he won't have that, apparently." Sue sighed. "I'll have to buy a new mould, but I'm running out of space to put them."

Ellie opened the cupboard where the moulds were stacked. She suddenly thought of the big trays that Ethan's mum had hired for the week. An idea coalesced in her mind. "Sue, why don't you hire the tins out."

"You what?"

"The cake moulds. You could hire the generic ones out to mums who want to make a nice cake for their kids, but don't want to buy a mould." She tried to think through what was involved. "You could charge them a deposit that was the cost of a new mould and when they bring the mould back, you give them the deposit back, minus the hire fee."

Sue straightened up and stared at her, thoughtfully. "You know, that's not a bad idea. They're sitting there anyway, taking up space."

"I could photograph each one and make up a folder. Maybe we could put a picture of the cakes you've made using the mould next to it to show people what they could do..."

"I like that," said Sue. She gave Ellie an appraising look. "Being away has given you a feel for new ideas," she said, approvingly.

Ellie flushed. "I don't know about that." She made her way past the counter. "I'll be off for my lunch then"

"On your way, can you take some more bread to the corner shop?" Sue pointed to the covered box. "Harriet called to say they've run out."

"On it." She grabbed the box and stepped outside. The summer sun beat down on her bare arms and shoulders as she walked up the street. It wasn't as hot as it had been in France, but it was pleasant. Better, even with a hint of breeze to cool things down. It was nice to be home.

The bell rang when she pushed open the door to the cornershop. It was a newsagent and all things shop rolled into one. There was no one behind the counter and for a second, Ellie felt like Ash was there. She approached the counter, half expecting him to pop out of the back room, book in hand.

"Hello?" she said. "I've brought the bread."

It wasn't Ash who appeared, which wasn't surprising, he was probably still in London. It was Harriet, who lived upstairs and sometimes minded the shop.

"Oh, how was France?" Harriet said. It seemed that everyone knew about her holiday. "Sophie's wedding go okay?"

"Yes thanks. It was lovely." She gave her a quick description of the wedding, leaving out anything about her and Ash, as she unpacked the bread and put it on the shelves.

"Did Ash behave himself?" Harriet was clearly joking, but Ellie felt her face heat up.

There was a second where Harriet's expression turned quizzical.

"I'd better get back," said Ellie. "I'll see you tomorrow, Harriet."

She ran out, flustered and confused by how she felt. Now Harriet probably thought that there was something going on between her and Ash. Which there wasn't. She was suddenly aware of the emptiness inside her, in the space that, for the past week, had been occupied by Ash's smile.

It was because she was so deep in thought, that she didn't spot the figure leaning against the wall opposite.

"Ellie!"

She snapped out of her reverie and realised she was looking at Luke.

"I thought I'd come join you for lunch," said Luke. He smiled at her and she waited for the familiar flip in her stomach. It didn't come. Well, that was interesting.

"So, how was it? Did you have fun on your little trip?" He put a hand on her elbow and steered her towards the church. She was too surprised to respond. The bench by the church was empty.

Luke sat down and gestured for her to join him. Ellie shook her head. He reached for her hand and pulled her towards him.

Being forced to sit down snapped her frozen brain into action. "Luke, what are you doing here?"

"Having lunch with my girl," he smiled at her. "What else?"

She scrambled back to her feet. "What? I'm not your girl anymore. We broke up."

"Aw, come on babe, that was just an argument. People have those all the time! We hadn't broken up." He beamed up at her.

Was it just an argument? She was pretty sure she'd dumped him. Had she, in her haste, been unclear about that? Is that why she'd felt so guilty?

"You had a thing you had to get out of your system. You wanted to go see your friend get married, and, fair enough, I should have been more understanding." He nodded, as though he was conceding something important. "But you went and you're back now. It's all good."

He pulled her back down to sit next to him. "We can go back to how things were. No harm, no foul."

"No harm-" She tried to get up, but he was still holding her arm. She could feel the roughness of his fingertips against the flesh on her upper arm. The feeling of apprehension that shot through her was disturbingly familiar. He wanted things to go back to how they had been and he wasn't having anything else. Ordinarily, she would have given in at this point. Well, not any more. She wasn't his girlfriend and she didn't have to put up with this anymore. "Luke. Let go of my arm."

He gave her a surprised look. "Okay," he said and made a show of releasing her, wriggling his fingers in the air. "Don't they hold hands in France?"

He was laughing at her. No wonder she'd felt guilty. She was so used to being controlled by him. He had been gaslighting her into thinking that what she wanted didn't matter. No wonder Ash's consideration of her feelings had freaked her out so much.

She stood up. "No, Luke." She took a few steps away and from the relatively safe distance, she said, "We're over. It wasn't just an argument. We weren't having a little break. It's over. I don't like the way you treat me and I don't want to be with you any more."

He was on his feet so fast, she felt another kick of fear. "Did you meet someone else when you were in France?" he demanded. "Have you been sniffing around other blokes as soon as my back was turned?"

Ellie took several steps back. "We are not together," she shouted. "I am single and I can do whatever the hell I like."

"So you did screw someone!" He was bellowing now.

Ellie turned and fled back to the tea shop, but Luke was faster. He grabbed her arm. "Answer me!"

"Luke, you're hurting me."

She wriggled, but he didn't release his grip. His nails dug into her arm. "Who was it?" he said. "Was it some Frenchman?" He spat the word out, and spittle sprayed in her face. For the first time, Ellie was genuinely afraid that he would hurt her. She struggled a bit more. "Luke. I'll scream."

"I can't believe I thought I loved you!" he shouted. "Slut!"

She kicked him, as hard as she could. Her foot connected with his shin and surprised him into letting go.

Ellie took her chance and made it to the shop.

Behind her, Luke spat out "Yeah, well you can fuck off, you lying cheating little bitch. You're dumped."

Sue shot out of the kitchen, drying her hands on a tea towel. "What's going on?" She marched up to the door and opened it. Luke might be a big lad, but Sue in full fury was a force to be reckoned with. He turned and marched down the street, still shouting obscenities.

Ellie's legs gave way and she collapsed into a chair and burst into tears.

Sue came back and leaned over her. "Are you alright, love?" She passed a napkin. Ellie nodded, then shook her head, then cried some more. She seemed to have lost the ability to form a coherent sentence.

Sue went away and a few minutes later, reappeared with a mug of tea. She sat down next to Ellie. "Here, drink this," she said. "Do you want to tell me what happened?"

It took a few minutes for Ellie to stop sobbing and collect her thoughts. She outlined what had happened. "I never thought he'd actually hurt me," she said.

"Let's see your arm."

She realised her arm was sore. When she lifted her arm, she saw the red finger marks. "Oh."

"That's going to bruise."

Ellie stared at it. All the conversations she'd had in the past with Sue about Luke came back to her. She had always defended him, but at some level she had known, hadn't she? It had taken his refusal to let her go to Sophie's wedding to make her see and it had taken a bruising for her to actually believe it.

"God, I'm such an idiot."

Sue gave her an oblique look. "No, you're not," she said. "Sometimes, it's hard to see it."

"It happened so gradually. He was different when we started going out. He just got more and more..." Ellie shook her head. "The worst thing is that I believed that it was all I was worth and when I met someone who treated me well, I sabotaged it."

Sue's eyes widened. "Wait, who is this? When did that happen?"

She had said too much. Her face flamed. "It's nothing," she said, quickly.

Someone knocked on the door to the cafe. Ellie looked over and noticed, for the first time, that Sue had turned the sign to say 'Closed'. Margie was knocking.

"I'll let her in," said Sue. "Don't think you've got away without telling me about this mystery man."

"You should open the shop again," Ellie said. "It's nearly lunchtime."

Sue unlocked the door and turned the sign back around.

"Everything alright?" said Margie.

"Yes." Sue came back and sat down again. "Ellie was about to tell us about this mystery man she met in France. Weren't you, Ellie."

"Oooh." Margie sat on the other side of her. "Tell all. I saw your ex marching off earlier, muttering and swearing. You're better off without him, I can tell you."

Ellie sighed. She may as well. They wouldn't rest until she told them. "It's not a mysterious man," she said. "It's Ash."

"Who's Ash?" said Margie.

"You know, Ash. Works in the cornershop in the holidays."

"What, young Ashanka? Quiet lad. Reads a lot?"

Ellie nodded. "That's him. He was at Sophie's wedding. We spent a lot of time together ..." Her cheeks warmed. "But I pushed him away. I felt it was too soon after Luke and ..." Fresh tears threatened. "I ruined it. He was a friend and I lost that too." She put her face in her hands. "I'm such a mess."

Chapter 16

Ellie went home early that day. Sue allowed her to, partly because she'd had a hard day, but partly because they both knew there was a chance that Luke might turn up at home time and it was best that she was already gone by then.

She expected the house to be empty, but her father's coat was handing up in its hook. "Dad?" she shouted up the stairs. "It's just me."

Dad appeared at the top of the stairs. "You're home early, lass. Everything okay?"

She was about to brush it all off with 'fine', but thought better of it. "Been better actually." She started up the stairs.

Dad backed up a bit to give her some space. "What's wrong?"

Ellie stopped and stared. He was wearing a shirt, neatly tucked into his good trousers. His hair was damp and he smelled of aftershave. He never made this level of effort to go to the pub.

"You look nice," she said, warily.

"Um…" he looked slightly panicked. "I'm going out tonight. I told you."

"Not to the pub, I take it?"

He reddened slightly.

Ellie bit back a smile and folded her arms. "Dad, is there something you need to tell me?"

For a second, he looked like he was going to shut down and storm off.

Ellie grinned. "Have you got a date, dad?"

He sighed, the tension draining out of him. "Would you be okay, if I had?"

What? Was he asking her permission? "Of course, I'd be okay. I'd be delighted. Who is she? Is she nice?" And, because she'd never known her dad to be anywhere other than in front of the TV or in the pub with his mates, she said, "And how long has this been going on?"

He was suddenly busy with his cuffs. "A few days," he said, to his hands. "You know your Aunt Jane's friend Shirley?"

She knew Shirley. Widowed a few years ago.

"Well, she asked me … and with you being away, I thought why not. So we met for a drink… one thing led to another and now I'm taking her out to dinner …" He looked up at her, his forehead crinkled with worry. "Are you sure you don't mind? If you need me for anything-"

"Dad. I'm so happy for you." She touched his arm. "Why did you think I'd mind?"

He sighed. "When your mum left, you didn't want me to leave you. You were so worried I wouldn't come back."

"But that was ages ago. I've grown up now."

"But I wasn't sure, was I. You're always my little girl and I didn't want to make things worse for you."

She stared at him and remembered the nights that she'd clung to him, crying. The times he's slept on the floor of her room because she'd had nightmares. The times they'd argued when she wanted to stay out. Wherever she went, she always knew where he was. On top of everything else that had happened today, it was too much. Her lip trembled. "Oh Dad."

"Oh no, love. Don't cry." He sounded panicked again. He put a hesitant arm around her, something he hadn't done in years. "I won't go."

"No, no, dad. It's not that. I'm glad you've found someone. I've just realised that I'm the reason you've been single all this time. I'm so sorry."

He put his other arm around her. She wiped her eyes and rested her forehead against his shoulder. He seemed smaller than she remembered. Or maybe it was just that she'd grown. She just hadn't stopped to take notice before.

"So ... you're okay with me going to see Shirley?" he said.

"Of course I am! It's great that you've got someone. I worry about you being lonely." She sniffed and pushed away. "Where are you taking her?"

"Thai place in Todmorden." He looked at his watch.

"Well you'd better get a move on, then," she said. "If you're going to pick her up from town, traffic will be murder soon."

Her dad laughed. "Aye." He patted her shoulder one last time. "Don't wait up for me."

She smiled back. "I won't." Then, as he started down the stairs, she said, "You look great."

He looked at her through the banister rails. "Thanks, love."

AFTER HER FATHER HAD gone, Ellie went downstairs and locked the door. She made herself some cheese on toast and ate it standing up in the kitchen, keeping a wary eye on the door, in case Luke showed up. Once she'd eaten, she double checked the locks on the door and took a cup of tea upstairs. Her phone rang. Luke's name flashed up on her screen. She dismissed the call mid-ring and blocked his number. Although he rarely contacted her through social media, she systematically unfriended and blocked him there too. She had never thought he would be bullying or vindictive, but then, she clearly didn't know him very well.

Lying on her bed, she scrolled through the Instagram posts from when she was on holiday. Helene had tagged her in a bunch of new pictures. Since Helene was behind the camera, Ellie and Ash appeared together in some of the photos. Sitting next to each other at the long meal table; hanging bunting up on trees; sitting in the sun on the riverbank.

She stopped at a photo taken the day they went to the river. They were in the restaurant, Ash pouring cola into a glass. She was next to him, caught in motion as she laughed, hair splayed across her face. Ash was smiling, his eyes were on her and his expression was so full of fondness that her eyes teared up all over again.

How could she be so stupid? First to think that Luke was the real thing and secondly to think that Ash was not. She laid the phone against her chest and stared at the ceiling. She remembered the terror of meeting 'foreigners'. These people that her dad distrusted because one man had hurt him and Luke distrusted for no good reason at all. Ellie had been ambivalent about it most of her life - after all, she didn't know many foreign people. Except now she knew people and she liked them. Oh, she and Helene didn't have that much in common, but if Helene were to ever visit England, Ellie would happily meet her and take her sightseeing. Tomas too. Luke had been wrong about Europeans. What else had he been wrong about?

Her plans had always been to stay in Trewton Royd to look after her dad and to be with Luke. But now, Luke was out of the picture... and Dad had got himself a girlfriend. He didn't need looking after either. All the certainties that had glued her life together had gone. She would have expected it to be terrifying. But it wasn't. She prodded her phone back to life and looked at the photo again. What would Ash do? She frowned. She was doing it again, looking to someone else to tell her what she wanted. What did she want? She stared at the ceiling. What did she want?

She had treated Ash badly and she felt terrible about that. No amount of apologising would take away the hurt in his voice when he scrambled out of the tent that night. But she could make an effort to keep in touch. She found his number and started writing a text. He had said he didn't want to be friends. She deleted what she'd written. But if she lost touch with him ... she could never get him back. And she very much wanted to get him back. She missed him. But then, maybe she was just missing having someone. If today had taught her any-thing, it was that she didn't know herself very well. Everything she'd thought was somehow tied up in her dependence on Luke and her dad. If she was going to be with Ash, she had to be very sure she wasn't going to turn him away again.

She sighed and put her phone away.

SHE WOKE UP IN THE night with a start. It was dark. There was a noise from downstairs. Ellie sat bold upright in bed, wondering if Luke had somehow let himself into the house. Then she heard humming. It was her dad, humming to himself as he came up the stairs.

Ellie sat on the edge of her bed and listened as Dad hummed and sang softly to himself as he got ready for bed. He sounded happy. She smiled and felt happy for him. He had been alone, devoted to Ellie, for a long time. He deserved to be happy. Still smiling, she went back to sleep.

SHE DIDN'T TEASE DAD very much the next morning. He wasn't given to cheeriness, but he wasn't actively scowling, which meant he was in a good mood.

"I'm staying late tonight, to help Sue finish a cake order," she told him. "I've got to make up a lot of hours. She advanced me two weeks wages so that I could go away."

"That was nice of her."

"She said it would be good for me to get out and see the world a bit," she said, cautiously.

He looked up from where he was buttering toast and then looked away again. "Well, now you're back," he said. "We can get on with life."

They ate sitting at the small table.

"How does Luke feel about you working late? You haven't seen each other in a week," he said, after a minute.

Ellie had a mouthful of toast and couldn't reply. She frowned.

Her dad leaned forward, "Listen love, I've been thinking. You'll be moving out to live with Luke soon and ..."

Ellie gulped down her mouthful and nearly choked. "I won't be moving out to live with Luke," she said, heart rate suddenly rising. "We split up."

"But when I saw Luke last week, he said-"

Oh god. "What did he say?"

Dad looked properly confused now. "He said you had a small argument, but you were fine. He thought you going to Sophie's wedding was a nice way for you to spend some time with your best friend before you started your own married life."

"No, we'd split up before I left. I was definitely clear about that." Ellie rubbed her temples with her fingertips, completely forgetting that she had butter on them. When she realised, she got up to some paper towel and rub her forehead. "Luke is having trouble letting go."

"Are you sure?" Her father twisted round in his seat. "Why've you broken up with him? Is it just because he didn't want you to go on holiday? I can't say I blame him. I mean look at what happened to your mother."

Ellie scrunched up the paper towel and threw it in the bin. "He's not good for me, Dad. He takes me for granted. He tells me how I should dress, what I should believe, how I should think. I thought he was ... well, anyway, I was wrong. He's a bully."

Dad stared at her. "What brought this on? He's always been good enough for you before. He's a nice lad-"

"No, dad. That's just it. He is not a nice lad."

He looked like he was going to argue. Not surprising. He liked Luke. They shared the same views about everything.

Ellie sighed and slipped off her cardigan. The bruise on her arm was now clearly a set of fingers and a thumb.

Dad's face clouded. "Did he do that?" he demanded. "I'm going to bloody kill him. How long has this been going on?" He got to his feet. "What didn't you tell me he was hitting you? I'll bloody murder him."

She put her hands up and stopped him. "No. He's never hurt me before. It was just yesterday. He tried to make me think that I was imagining breaking up with him. And when I didn't go with what he said, he got rough. It was just the once."

Dad stared at the bruises on her arm. "Just the once," he said, faintly.

"But I think once is enough, don't you?"

He nodded. He seemed to shrink a little before her eyes. "He did that to you," he whispered. "I've tried so hard to protect you. And I let that man into this house."

"It's not your fault," said Ellie. "You weren't to know. I didn't know. And technically, I let that man into this house."

"I'm sorry, Ellie. I'm meant to be the one who looks after you." He looked confused. Lost.

"I'm a grown woman now though, Dad. You don't need to look after me. To be honest, I thought I was looking after you."

"You what?"

"I mean, I cook all the meals and help you keep the house..."

"I suppose you do," he said. Suddenly, he pulled her into a fierce hug. "I don't know what I'd do without you."

Ellie squeezed him back. "Maybe spend more time with Shirley?" she said.

Emotions flitted across his face. Embarrassment, annoyance, love.

"Oh, come on," said Ellie. "Aunt Jane's right. It's time you went out and had some fun."

"But what about you?"

She thought of Ash. "It's time I got used to being myself. See who I am without Luke."

"I don't want you to end up alone, love."

She thought of Ash again. If someone clever like Ash could like her, then perhaps someone else could too. "I'll be fine, dad."

Chapter 17

"What the bloody hell happened with you and Ash?" It was a week after the wedding and Sophie was on the phone. She had started yelling the minute Ellie answered the phone.

"Oh, hi Soph. How was the honeymoon?" Ellie, who had been getting ready for bed, climbed in and pulled the covers up over her legs.

"Never mind that. What happened? When I left, you and Ash were together and when I texted him this morning, he said he didn't want to talk about it. What's going on? What did he do?"

"Nothing. He didn't do anything."

"Then what did you do?"

When she didn't reply, Sophie continued, "You guys are perfect for each other."

Ellie frowned. "Why?"

"What do you mean, why? Just look at the two of you! It's so obvious you fancied the pants off each other. How did it go wrong overnight?"

Ellie sighed and tweaked the duvet to block a small draught against her shins. "Ash is nice," she said. A twinge in her chest made her add, "more than just nice". She sighed. "But I wasn't ready to go out with anyone. I had some stuff I needed to figure out and I couldn't lead him along. It wouldn't be fair."

"So you used him and dumped him?" Sophie sounded horrified. "Who are you and what have you done with my lovely friend?"

"A lot has happened, okay, Soph."

"Okay then, tell me." Sophie sounded calmer now. "What's happened?"

Ellie outlined what had happened with Luke when she got home, and her conversations with dad. "So, I'm not totally sure who I am anymore. All that stuff I believed just because Luke or dad said so. I mean, what do I believe? I thought I wanted to live with Luke and have his babies and never leave Trewton. But now, I know there's so much more that I can do. I mean, at your wedding, I could almost have a conversation in French by the end. I never thought I could do that!"

Sophie gave a tiny laugh. "That's because that bell end Luke has spent the last four years telling you that you're stupid. You're really not."

Ash had said the same thing. "I know. I ..." Ellie sighed. She had been trying so hard to be strong. To show her dad that she was okay with him moving on, to hold her head up when customers said 'I heard you split up with that Luke'; to not think about Ash and how he made her feel. It was exhausting.

"Ellie, are you okay?"

She sighed again. "Yes. Just a bit ... You know, it's hard. All this adulting."

"I can imagine. Listen, I'm sorry I was cross with you. The last thing you need right now is me telling you who I think you should be with."

"How is he?"

Sophie understood who she meant. "He's not a happy bunny, really," she said. "I think, coming on top of what happened with his ex-"

Ellie winced.

"He genuinely liked you Ells and he's pretty cut up about it not working out."

"He was so polite and distant on the way home."

"That's what Ash does. Quiet and polite is how he is when he's with people he doesn't know. It takes him a while to come out of his shell. It was so nice to see him relax with you in France. I was so keen to get you two together, that I didn't think of the possibility of him getting hurt."

"Oh, Sophie."

"Ellie, can I ask you? Do you like him? I know you fancied him, that was obvious, but do you like him? You know, in the future, when you've got sorted out, would you try again?"

Ellie closed her eyes and thought of the way Ash's face lit up when she walked in. Of the way her stomach fluttered at the sound of his laugh. The way she felt comfortable with him in a way she hadn't been with Luke. "Yes," she said. "I would. But it's too late, isn't it? I hurt him in the worst way I could have. He must hate me."

Sophie made a non-committal sound. "Maybe not," she said. "He's hurt, sure. But if you talk to him ... make some sort of gesture..."

"Like what?"

"I don't know, Ellie. You'll have to work that one out on your own. Once you've worked out whether you really want to."

They talked some more and Sophie finally told Ellie the highlights of her honeymoon holiday. When Ellie finally hung up, she felt better than she had in years. She looked at the phone in her hand. Sometime during the conversation, she had made up her mind. She did want to see Ash again. It wouldn't be like it was with Luke. He wasn't in the village all the time. She might have to go down to London to see him - but she'd done train and bus journeys alone now. She knew she could. And maybe not living in each other's pockets would be a good way to be in a relationship.

But first, she needed to fix the damage she'd done.

It took a few goes to work out what to say. In the end, the text she sent said 'I'm sorry. I was wrong. Please can we talk?'

She put the phone down, hopped out of bed to go brush her teeth, so that she could turn in properly. Without Luke to take up her time, and Dad out with Shirley twice a week, her evenings seemed longer now. So much so that she'd popped out when the library bus came round and now had a rom com to read. She had forgotten how relaxing reading was. Almost better than TV.

She had only read a couple of pages when the phone rang, making her jump and almost drop her book. The screen said Ash. She answered it. "Hi."

"Hi." He sounded hesitant. "You ... said you wanted to talk..."

"Oh. Yes. I ... oh god, Ash, I'm so sorry. I didn't mean to hurt you like that."

"You said."

"I didn't use you. I really, genuinely did like you... do like you. I was just so messed up."

"You used me, Ellie. You needed a rebound guy and I was convenient." He didn't sound angry, just tired and so, so polite.

"I honestly didn't think I was. I don't expect you to understand, but the thing with Luke was ... complicated and it ran deeper than even I knew. I liked you, but I didn't feel I deserved to be liked back, if that makes any sense."

He cleared his throat. "I'm not sure it does."

"Look, Ash. Can we be friends? I understand that it's too much to ask for anything more than that. But friends? Please?"

There was such a long silence, that she wondered if the connection had dropped out. "Ash? Are you still there?"

"Yes. I'm here." He sighed. "Okay. Let's start again. Friends."

"Brilliant."

There was an awkward silence. Now they'd got over that, what next? Her gaze fell on the book lying in her lap. Suddenly, she knew exactly what to talk about. "Oh," she said. "Guess what I'm reading?"

Chapter 18

en months later

Ellie and Sue worked quietly in the back of the shop, Sue making sugar craft toppings for cakes and Ellie making a shepherd's pie. The cafe was closed now.

Ellie left the pan simmering and took out the baking tray that the customer had left. It was quite a nice Denby one. "I like this," she said. "They're much nicer than the Le Creuset baking dishes that some people have. Those things are so heavy."

"They're good pans though." Sue put scales onto tiny mermaid tails using an icing tool.

"Most of them look like they've never been used." She got to see a lot of baking dishes now. After the cake tin loan scheme took off, Ellie came up with the idea of doing tray baked meals for people. She already had her food hygiene certificates, so Sue let her try advertising the service. It was when she suggested that people could bring their own baking dishes in and Ellie would make meals in their own dishes, so that they could pretend they'd made it themselves, that the idea really took off. Someone told their NCT group and soon there was a steady stream of orders for Ellie's 'home cooked' meals. It got to the point where she had to ask people to give her three days' notice, four if they had special dietary requirements.

It was Tuesday, which meant she had only one meal to prepare. The weekends were another matter entirely.

She checked the pan of potatoes, which were nearly cooked. Her phone, which she'd left in her coat, rang. Frowning, she cleaned her hands and picked it up.

Ash's name came up on the screen. She put it on speakerphone. "Hi Ash, I'm at work."

"What still?" he said. "You work late!"

"You're on speakerphone," she added, meaningfully.

Sue shouted, "Hello. Don't mind me."

"Oh, hi ...er ... Sue."

"I can't really talk long," said Ellie. "I've got some potatoes which are nearly done."

He didn't ask for details. She'd told him all about her ideas. In fact, if it hadn't been for his encouragement, she probably wouldn't have plucked up the courage to ask Sue about setting up the evening catering service. "Actually, it'll only take a minute," Ash said. "I'm coming up for a job interview tomorrow, which means I'll be home tomorrow evening. Did you fancy going for a drink with me and the lads?"

Ellie's gaze flicked to the order chart. Tomorrow was actually doable. "Sure," she said. "If Sue doesn't need me."

Sue waved her away.

"Um... yes. That would be lovely," Ellie said, to the phone. "Shall I meet you at the Trewton Arms then?"

"Eightish?"

"Eightish works for me."

"Great. I'll see you tomorrow, then," said Ash. "Night Sue!"

They both chorused "Bye," and Ellie hung up. She put the phone back and went to wash her hands again before getting back to work. She could sense Sue's eyes on her back.

"What?" she said.

Sue raised her eyebrows. "What's going on there, then?"

"Nothing." Ellie turned the heat off from under the potatoes. "We're just friends." Which was a pity in some ways, but that was all he wanted from her now. She had properly messed that up.

"Is that enough, just being friends?" Sue was sharper than was good for anyone.

Ellie picked up the potato pan and hefted it over to the sink to drain it. "Yeah, it's enough," she said into the cloud of steam. Her face felt hot. She told herself it was because of the steam.

Sue went back to her work. "So, when did you last see him?" She didn't look up.

Ellie rolled her eyes. "I haven't seen him since last year. We talk every so often. Like I said, we're friends."

"How many of your friends do you talk to every couple of weeks?" Sue said.

Sophie didn't call so often now that she was married. Ellie spoke to Ash more often than she spoke to Sophie. Not that she was keeping track.

When she didn't reply, Sue said, "See. He means something to you, love. More than a friend." She put down her icing bag. "I'm just saying that I wasted twenty years being stubborn and not talking to Jack. If he hadn't come back to find me, we'd still be like that. It sounds to me like you and Ash have something special going. It'd be a shame to let that die because you're too scared to take it any further."

"I'm not the one who's too scared," Ellie snapped. She realised what she'd just said and groaned.

"Oh," said Sue. "Oh, Ellie, I'm sorry. I didn't realise. Had you ... talked about it?"

"We did, but only briefly. I hurt him and he didn't want to risk getting hurt again." She sighed. "And he was right. I needed some time to remember how to be myself. Last year I was still trapped thinking about being Luke's girl."

"Not now though," said Sue. "Look at you. You've expanded the range of this shop. You've gone from the occasional shop girl to being a full time employee. You're a business woman now."

Ellie shook her head. "Who lives with her dad." She began mashing the potatoes to go on the top of the shepherd's pie.

"Well, you can't have everything," said Sue. "At least, you're not running around looking after your dad so much now."

She still cooked a lot of his meals and cleaned the house, but yes, they were more like housemates now. Dad spent a couple of nights a week over at Shirley's house. Those were Ellie's favourite nights, because she could put a face mask on and watch whatever cheesy telly she liked.

"Why don't you see how tomorrow goes," said Sue, gently. "He's had a year to get over it. If he's chatting to you of an evening, he's clearly not averse to you... things might have changed with him too."

"I don't know, Sue. He's got his degree. He's going to do some sort of law training. He'll get a high flying job in that London... I don't see how it's going to work." She shook her head. And then there was dad. He wouldn't approve. But then again, she didn't need him to.

Someone knocked on the door. Sue wiped her hands and opened the side door that led into the kitchen. "Oh, hello." The joy in her voice was enough to tell Ellie that it was Jack at the door. There was a muffled giggle from the back. Yes, it was definitely Jack. He was the only person who could turn the normally ultra-sensible Sue into a giggler.

"Hi Jack!" Ellie called.

Professor Jackson Bruce, Sue's long lost and now reunited boyfriend came into the kitchen proper. "Hello Ellie," he said. He sounded southern, but there was the slightest hint of the north in his accent. Sue said it was stronger here than it was when he was in Reading, where he lived.

"I'll be another half hour or so," said Sue. "You should have called first."

"Not a problem," said Jack. "I'll just sit here quietly and wait." He took a seat behind the counter and pulled a book out of his pocket.

"What are you reading?" Ellie said, almost out of reflex.

"*The Handmaid's Tale.*"

"I haven't read that one," said Ellie. "I'm scared to. I've read *The Blind Assassin*, though."

"Oh, me too," Jack said. "Thoroughly enjoyed that. I'm enjoying this too ... I think."

Sue shook her head. "Listen to you bookworms," she said.

Ellie smiled and got on with ladling shepherd's pie mix into the customer's baking dish and covering it with a good layer of potato. It amused her to be called a bookworm. She would never have considered herself to be one, which was strange because she did like to read or listen to audio books. She had stopped reading books in public when she was a teenager, but she'd carried on listening to A Book at Bedtime on the radio. Luke had found the radio annoying, so she'd turn it off when he was around, which became more and more often, until she stopped bothering altogether. Ash nudging her to start reading again had reminded her of the joy of escaping into different worlds and with Luke gone, she had more time to herself. Instead of finding time to get bored, she was now busier than she ever was, in between work and reading and thinking about ways to improve the business. Having spent her teens being terrified of finding herself single, she was now finding she loved it.

Once she'd finished the Shepherd's pie she disappeared to the back to deal with the pans. The dishwasher was still running the load from the day. Sometimes it was easier to just wash up by hand rather than wait.

She put the pie in the pantry to cool. "That's me done," she said, as she went back into the kitchen. "Is there anything you need me to do?"

The mermaid tails were done. Sue fetched the torsos she'd made earlier and started to join them up and add faces to them. "Could you make up a batch of buttercream, please love?"

It didn't take long to whip that up. Soon Ellie was standing next to Sue, deftly adding waves of blue buttercream to the cupcakes, so that Sue could put the mermaids on them when she'd finished with them.

The swirls of icing made her think of Ash, painstakingly adding swirls of cream onto scones. Whenever she spoke to Ash, for a few days afterwards, everything reminded her of him. It was annoying and comforting in equal parts. Maybe she was just using her memories of him to keep herself from getting lonely. It had been a year. When she saw him the next night, she might find that all the physical chemistry between them had been eroded away by time. Yeah. That was the most likely thing.

She didn't want to think about how she'd feel if that were true.

ELLIE GOT HOME AND unpacked the Tupperware containers she'd brought back from the shop. One contained a few broken cakes and biscuits and the other contained the spare bits of shepherd's pie and mash, which they could have for their dinner.

Her dad came in from the front room, where the TV was still on. "Oh, you're back," he said. "I was starting to think that I'd have to make myself cheese on toast again."

She pushed the shepherd's pie mix towards him. "Here. You have this."

He looked at it dubiously. "I'm not sure there's enough here for two."

"You have it all. I'll just have some toast." She was tired. All she wanted to do was to have a shower and curl up in bed with her latest book. "No Shirley tonight?"

"She's gone out for a friend's birthday." Her dad put the container in the microwave and watched as she put the kettle on. "Sue works you too hard," he said.

"No, I work me too hard," said Ellie. "I run the catering side of things. I know it's part of Sue's business, but I run it." He knew this, of course, but he kept forgetting. It was almost as though he didn't believe she could be a businessperson.

"What do you get for it, eh?" he said.

"Well, a share of the takings and a pension plan." She didn't want to talk about this now. She and Sue had discussed what she needed and they'd come to the conclusion that she should stay as Sue's employee, with all the benefits that brought. Essentially, Sue had promoted her in return for her adding an extra income stream to Pat's Pantry. She was saving up what she could, but she had increased the amount of rent she paid to her dad.

The microwave pinged. He got the container out, sat down and dug in with a fork, not bothering to plate it out. "What're you up to tonight?"

Ellie tipped her head back against the cupboards. "Toast. Shower, then probably go to bed and read."

"Read eh? Not talk to that friend of yours?"

"Ash? No, he's got a job interview tomorrow."

Dad made a 'humph' noise and went back to eating. She could feel the disapproval coming off him.

Ellie raised her head. "What?"

He sighed. "I don't like him hanging around you like that, that's all."

"What?!" She knew why. She didn't really want to think about it.

"I mean, he clearly thinks he's got a chance with you. And you're leading him on," her father continued.

"I'm not leading him on," she said, wearily.

"You are. Talking to him at all hours. Laughing. I heard you."

"Dad. I'm not leading him on. I genuinely like him." Behind her, the toast popped. She turned, but didn't miss the astonishment on her father's face.

"But. But you can't," he said. "He's foreign."

She spun round. "Foreign?" she spat out. "He was born in Halifax. He went to primary school just over the hill. He went to the same secondary school as me and he went to university in bloody Staffordshire. Which bit of that is foreign?"

His face had gone red. "His family are foreign. They go back there on holidays."

"Going somewhere doesn't make you foreign. I went to France for a holiday. I didn't come back French, did I?" She opened the drawer and took out a butter knife.

"You came back with some bloody funny ideas though!"

Ellie spun round and slapped the knife down on the table. The crash of metal on wood rang through the kitchen. "Like what, dad?" She was shouting now. "Like what?"

Before he could answer, she leaned across the table. "Like thinking that I didn't need a man to complete me? Like believing that I wasn't as stupid as you and Luke made out I was? Like realising that I can do better than being a waitress all my life? Things like that?"

He scowled and crossed his arms. "Well, it wouldn't hurt you to find a proper man, would it? You're lonely. You're getting funny ideas about unsuitable men because you're lonely."

"Dad. I am not a child anymore. I can fancy whoever the fuck I like."

"Not in my bloody house you don't!"

She stared at him, too shocked to respond. The atmosphere in the kitchen dropped to freezing. For a moment all she could hear was her own breathing and the tinny remnants of sound from the telly. She couldn't believe he'd just said that. At the same time, it seemed inevitable.

He broke first. "I'm sorry," he said. "I didn't mean that."

"Didn't you, though?" she said. Drawing a deep breath, she straightened up. "I'm going to have a shower. Good night." She walked out of the kitchen.

"What about your toast?"

"You have it. I'm not hungry."

She marched up the stairs. This row with her father had been long overdue. For a while, it had looked like his relationship with Shirley might change things, but they'd settled into a new pattern instead. Twice a week, Ellie had the house to herself while Dad went over to Shirley's, but apart from that, life settled back into its usual routine.

He still thought of Ellie as the docile, naive girl who needed to be looked after. He was still convinced that Ellie had to get married to be off his hands. He assumed that she'd stay in Trewton Royd. Nothing would change. But last summer had changed her. It had shown her a life outside of the box she'd put herself in. There was no way she could go back. And if Dad couldn't support her in that, she'd have to move out.

At the back of her mind, numbers whirred. She had several months of savings. She already paid rent here. That rent could just as well be paid out to someone else. Maybe it was time she took the next step.

Chapter 19

Ellie was late getting to the pub and arrived a little flustered. She paused in the entranceway to catch her breath, before she pushed open the door that led to the bar. The Trewton Arms was an old fashioned sort of pub, with low beams and faded furniture. Phil, the landlord, waved a hand in greeting. Since she'd been delivering the baked goods to the pub every morning since she was fourteen, Ellie knew the pub very well. She had even done the odd Sunday cleaning shift when the place was busy in the summer.

She didn't spot Ash immediately, so she walked past the bar and peered into the room with the pool table in it. Three men were there - two playing, the third was Ash. He was leaning against the windowsill, pint of beer in hand. She heard his laugh across the pub and felt it punch through all her defences. Her heart sped up and the butterflies in her stomach went mad. Oh dear. This wasn't going to go well.

She retreated to the bar and ordered a white wine spritzer. When she had come in with Luke, he had always ordered her a half of beer, which was what she'd asked for the first time she'd been out with him. He assumed that's what she'd want and she'd never thought to ask for something different. Now, she did. She had tried a variety of different drinks in the last year. White wine spritzer was next on her list.

"You alright, love?" Phil said. "You look a bit worried."

"No. No, it's just been a long day, that's all. I'm meeting some friends for a drink. I think a break will do me good." She took a sip of her drink, partly to stop herself from babbling.

Phil gave her a puzzled smile and handed over the change. "You have a good night, love."

"Cheers Phil." She took a deep breath and made her way over to the back.

When he saw her, Ash's face lit up. She felt a wild swing of happiness. He was pleased to see her. That was a good sign wasn't it?

He pushed himself away from the windowsill and took a step towards her. "Hi."

"Hello." This was awkward. They spoke to each other regularly, but they hadn't seen each other for a year. She wondered if she should kiss him on the cheek. She wasn't sure she could handle that.

Ash solved it for her by saying, "It's so good to see you," and patting her awkwardly on the shoulder.

The other two guys stopped their game of pool.

"You know Max and James, right?" Ash said.

She knew who they were. They had all gone to the same school. "Hi. You alright?"

They both mumbled that they were fine, glanced at Ash and went back to their game of pool.

Ellie followed Ash back to where there was a table and stools. She sat down and he sank down next to her, both facing the pool table.

"So," she said. "How've you been?"

He gave her an amused look. "You know how I've been."

"Yes, but ... now that I've seen you, I don't know what to say." She took a sip of her drink. "This is so weird."

He winced as Max missed a shot. "Well, how was your day?"

"Same old, same old, really." Her brain kicked into gear. "Oh, how did the job interview go?"

Instead of replying, he grinned at her. Happiness seemed to beam out of him.

"Oh," she said. "You got a job!"

"They called me when I was on the train back and offered it to me."

She wanted to hug him. But she didn't know how he'd take it. She punched him lightly in the arm instead. "That's wonderful, congratulations. You should have told me."

"I wanted to surprise you." He looked down at his drink.

"You certainly achieved that."

They sat in silence for a few minutes. There was a weird sinking feeling in Ellie's stomach. After all those days of Messenger comments and gifs and photos of passages from books, now that they actually saw each other, they had nothing to say.

"I went to the bookshop yesterday," he said.

"I know." She had seen the photo of his book haul. Some of them, she would have liked to read.

"I've finished one already." He proceeded to tell her about it.

She asked questions and soon, they were talking again. The guys finished their game and had to surrender the table to someone else. They came to join them.

"What do you think?" Ash asked Max. "Do you think the prequel to the Hunger Games is going to be a thinly disguised allegory of American politics in the past four years?"

"Probably," Max said. "We live in dystopian times."

After that, the evening improved. The guys, it turned out, were nice. Luke had always sneered at the nerds and Ellie had never bothered getting to know them. She regretted that now. James was very interested in her catering operation.

"So you cook stuff for people in their own dishes, so that they can pretend they made it themselves? That's mad."

Ellie swallowed a sip of her drink. "Most people don't bother pretending they made it. It's convenient and they like being able to use their own dishes. It's more environmentally friendly than foil trays and they get to use the good dishes that they got as wedding presents or whatever." She shrugged. "It's basically what they'd do themselves if they had the time."

James nodded, slowly. "That's genius."

Ellie felt her cheeks redden. "It's not that great-" she began, but Ash interrupted her. "It is genius," he said. "It hits an underserved section of the market. Busy people who want to be able to cook nice, healthy meals at home, but for whatever reason, don't have time. Now they get to have a meal cooked for them every so often without it being a takeaway. It's brilliant. You shouldn't diminish that."

No, she shouldn't. She felt a glow of pride. He was right. It was clever and she had thought of it all by herself. He had helped her think of all the angles so that she could cost it properly before she talked to Sue, but apart from that, it was all her idea. She should own that. "Thanks," she said.

"So, what sort of meals do you do?" said James, tapping away on his phone. "Do you have a card or a website or something?"

"There's a Facebook page. Look for Pat's Pantry, Trewton Royd," Ellie said. She had set that up too. She leaned across and pointed. "If you look at the side bar, you'll see the menu."

"Ah brilliant." James' fingers danced over the screen. "I'm sending this to my girlfriend. She and I take turns to cook. We normally get takeaway on a Friday because we're both knackered by then. This could be a better alternative."

It was, overall, a lovely evening. Ellie kept sneaking glances at Ash, remembering the joy of being with him that summer, knitting together the physical memories with the long drawn out emotional memories they'd made by being just friends. He had been so clear that he didn't want anything more than friendship, that he was bound to freak out if she made any kind of move on him now. He watched him push up his sleeves and the memory of being held in those arms made her feel weak at the knees.

How could she have thought that she loved Luke more than she could love Ash? A good man had been offered to her on a plate and she'd turned him down because she was so damned insecure. Well, she wasn't that girl now. Sue had said she was almost a different person. Maybe now was the time to put that to good use.

She looked at her phone. "I'm sorry guys, I'm going to have to go. I have an early start at the bakery tomorrow."

"Do they still do those cinnamon buns?" said Max, suddenly. "I love those."

"We do." Ellie stood up and picked up the jacket she'd hung on the back of her chair. "You should come round and grab one, sometime."

"I will," said Max.

Ash stood too. "Do you need someone to walk you home?"

The other two men exchanged glances.

"Yes please," said Ellie. "That would be very kind."

"Sure." He nodded to his friends. "I'll see you guys later, right?"

"It was lovely to meet you guys again, James and Max. I'll just go to the loo, I'll meet you by the bar, Ash." She left them so that Ash could say his goodbyes in peace.

She came back out of the toilets to find Ash standing by the bar, on his phone. He looked up as she approached and grinned.

They walked out of the pub together. It was still early summer, so the night was cool and clear. The hills rose out of the valley, dark with distant street lights snaking through the blackness like liquid gold. They walked past the shops and turned just before the bridge to head towards Ellie's house.

The brook that ran through the village gurgled cheerfully from beyond the waist high wall that separated the road from the water. Just here, if you leaned over the wall, you could see the valley widen out and the brook gleaming in the moonlight. Ellie mentioned it, so Ash stopped to have a look.

"Ellie," he said, still looking out at the valley. "I actually have two job offers."

"Oh, that's brilliant. Do you know which one you'll choose?"

"Well ... one's in Sheffield, as you know. The other one's in London. The one down south is better paid."

Her heart sank. Of course he'd choose London. "Cost of living is higher down there."

"Even still, it's better."

"Right. Well. It's a no brainer then, isn't it?"

He sighed, still not looking at her.

So that was it. He was going to stay down south. She had hoped that he would come back... that they might rekindle something of what they'd had that summer. But no. Still. She was his friend. She had to be supportive. She put a hand on his arm and he flinched and looked down at her hand.

"Ellie," he said, still looking at her hand. "Do you remember, I said I wasn't sure we could be friends after what happened...?"

Oh god. He didn't even want to be her friend anymore. She let go of his arm and tucked her hands in her pockets. "Ash-"

He held up his own hand to stop her. "The thing is ... the last thing I think about at night is you. The first thing I do when I wake up is check if you've messaged me. I can't stop thinking about you, Ellie. When I said I didn't think I could be friends again, I was right. I can't just be friends. It's torture. I think I'm in love with you, Ellie. I-"

He couldn't say any more because she kissed him.

She must have taken him by surprise because he froze. A second later, he recovered and kissed her back. His arms wrapped around her and pulled her close. She felt like her heart would explode.

When they finally broke apart, he said, "Right then." Even in the weak glow of the streetlight, she could see him beaming. "So, I'm guessing you're okay with more than just friends."

She rested her head on his shoulder. "Ash... I thought you were going to break up with me just then. I thought I would die from the sadness of it."

His arms tightened around her. "I couldn't break up with you. We weren't going out."

"It felt like we were though, didn't it?"

"No ... it wasn't nearly enough." He kissed the top of her head.

No, it wasn't. Her body seemed to be waking up, responding to the proximity of his. She remembered all too well what it felt like to taste him, to feel the movement of muscles under her fingertips. Her house was only minutes away. "My dad's not at home tonight," she said out loud.

"Perhaps we should get you home, then?"

They started walking, with their arms round each other's waist.

"You know," said Ash. "Your dad is going to hate me."

"I know," she said. "But ... I am an adult and I can do whatever I want with whoever I want."

He was silent for a few minutes. The only sounds were the steady clump of their footsteps and the receding babble of the brook.

"Ellie. What exactly would you like to do ...?"

She laughed. "You'll see."

They reached the dark and silent house and she had to let go of him to let them in. Once they were in the hallway, he stood at the foot of the stairs and watched her carefully lock the door. She turned to look at him and her body responded with a fierce wave of lust. She stepped up to him. He smiled, took her hand and pulled her closer. "So."

She rested her forehead against his. "So."

He chuckled and kissed her. She wrapped her arms around his neck and pressed against him, kissing him back with all the need built up over the months of flirting by text. They stumbled up the stairs, and fell into her room, pulling clothes off each other as they went.

"I have condoms this time," she said, kicking the door shut.

"So do I." He pulled her down onto her bed.

Chapter 20

Three months later

Ellie picked up the last bag and looked around her room. These walls had seen her grow up. She glanced at the patches of wallpaper where her pictures had been blu-tacked up. If she looked carefully, she could see places where the posters from her childhood had once been. She wasn't taking any furniture with her. Dad and Shirley were probably going to keep this as a spare room. Maybe a place for her to come and stay when she came over. She felt a heavy weight in her chest to think that she was saying goodbye to it.

With a sigh, she hefted the bag onto her shoulder and went downstairs. Dad was waiting for her, his coat already on. "You ready love?"

Ellie nodded, her eyes prickled. She couldn't cry. Not after all the effort it had taken to convince dad that this was a good idea.

Shirley appeared from the kitchen, drying her hands on a tea towel. "Bye, Ellie love." She opened her arms and pulled her in for a hug.

Ellie hugged her back, awkward.

"I'll look after him, don't you worry," Shirley said.

Ellie smiled. "I know you will." From what she'd seen, Shirley genuinely liked her dad and he seemed to be a milder, happier man for having been with her. It was a relief to know that dad would have company when she'd gone. Ellie sniffed.

Dad wiped his eyes. "Come on," he said, gruffly. "Let's get you to this flat before the traffic gets too bad."

Ash had found a flat in a village between Trewton Royd and Sheffield. It was close enough to a train station that he could get into Sheffield and it was only a half hour drive in the opposite direction for Ellie to come to Trewton. It was as good a compromise as they were going to find.

She followed her dad out and got into the car.

"Are you sure about this?" he asked her, for what seemed like the hundredth time. "You've only been with him for three months. Are you sure you're not rushing it?" He didn't approve, but the mere fact that they'd stopped arguing about it told her that he was trying to give her more space.

"Dad, we've been together for so much longer than that. We just didn't want to admit it. I love him. And yes, I'm sure."

He sighed. "Fine. But if you change your mind, there's always a room here for you."

She wondered what Shirley would have to say about that. "Yes Dad, I know."

He took a deep breath, nodded and put the car into gear.

SHE ALREADY HAD A KEY, so Ellie let them in. Radio 4 played from the living room. She found Ash in the living room, unpacking books. He scrambled to his feet. "Hi." His eyes shone and she could almost read the happiness in them. "Hi Roy. Thanks for helping Ellie move."

Dad managed a gruff nod.

"Can I get you a drink?" Ash said. "I unpacked the kettle first. I'll have to wash up a mug, but-"

"No. Let's get our Ellie moved in first, shall we?"

They carried up her boxes. There weren't many. Her life had been so narrow, she hadn't accumulated much. The idea of her dad taking things into the new bedroom that she was going to share with Ash was too weird, so she asked them to dump her boxes in the living room. Neither Ash, nor dad commented on it.

When the last box was up, dad refused another offer for a cuppa and gave Ellie a hug. "You look after yourself," he said, into her hair. "If you need anything, anything at all, you call me. Okay?"

"I will Dad. I promise." She clung on to him for a few seconds, breathing in the familiar smell of him, holding on to the feel of his hug.

Dad let her go. He turned to Ash, who was standing nearby. "You." He pointed a finger at Ash. "You be good to my girl." It was part instruction, part plea.

Ash nodded, solemnly. "I will, Roy," he said. "I promise."

Ellie moved closer to him and took his hand.

Dad nodded. "Aye." He turned and walked to the door.

Ellie went after him. "Bye Dad," she said. "I love you."

When he turned, his eyes were full of tears. "My Ellie," he said.

This time she held him. "I'll be coming to Trewton every day, Dad. I work there, remember. If you want to see me, you can just pop in at lunchtime. Besides, you've got Shirley now.

You can't have a proper go at being with her with me under your feet, can you? You'll be reet."

He gave her an extra hard squeeze and left, wiping his eyes. Ellie watched him trudge down the stairs before she shut the door.

She went back to the living room, to find it empty. "Ash?"

"In here."

She found him in the kitchen. Making tea.

"Here." He handed her a mug. "I figure you probably need this."

Her gaze drifted around the kitchen and rested on a packet of pasta, and a bag of what looked like groceries on the surface. "What's this?"

He looked embarrassed. "I ... er... I thought I'd make you dinner. I know I'm not a great cook like you are, but I thought you might like ... you might like someone to cook for you for a change."

It was a small gesture, but one that hadn't been made for her before. She stared at the food, her lip trembling.

"Ellie?" Ash sounded faintly panicked. "Are you okay?"

She flung herself into his arms and kissed him. "I love you."

He gave her a bemused smile. "I love you too."

For a moment, she held him tightly. This was a big step for her and it terrified her. "I'm scared," she said to him.

"I know," he said. "Me too. But it's a good kind of scared, right?" He kissed the top of her head.

The last time she'd done something that scared her, it had changed everything. It had led her here. To this man. She lifted her head to look at him and he kissed her forehead.

"We can do this," he said. "We're proper grownups now."

She laughed and stroked his cheek. "We are, aren't we?" He kissed her again.

"Since we're adults," she said. "What say we go christen the bed?"

He laughed. "We'd have to find the bedlinen first."

She rolled her eyes. "Come on."

He grinned and kissed her. He walked her backwards, still kissing her, towards the bedroom. She tugged at his t-shirt and pulled it off him. He did the same with hers. They didn't quite make it to the bed.

The End

THANK YOU FOR READING *That Holiday in France*. If you enjoyed it, please leave a review at your favourite book retailer.

Thank you, thank you, thank you in advance!

Rhoda

WHAT TO READ NEXT

If you enjoyed *That Holiday in France* why not try the rest of the Trewton Royd series. They can all be read as standalone stories:

Pat's Pantry (short story) – Ellie makes her first appearance in this short story. Jack broke Sue's heart twenty years ago. And now he's back, but is Sue ready to forgive him?

SNOWED IN – Burned out tech millionaire Tracey and just-been-dumped lawyer Vinnie get trapped in a blizzard together. At Christmas time.

BELONGING – Ash first appears in this story. Harriet is still grieving when her late lover's teenage daughter turns up on her doorstep. Can helping the teenager move on help Harriet too?

CHRISTMAS FOR COMMITMENTPHOBES – Lara is too busy for romance and Tilly is not the sort to settle down. Can being forced to spend Christmas in the Trewton Arms change their minds?

Want a free Christmas novella?

Join my newsletter and get a Christmas novella absolutely free.

-BRITISH-ASIAN HEROINE

   -plus sized hero

   -set in a microbiology lab

   -Christmas

   To get your free copy, just go to my website www.rhodabaxter.com, where a sign up link is available.

Other Books by Rhoda Baxter

TREWTON ROYD SMALL town romance novellas - All can be read as standalone stories

PAT'S PANTRY - short story

SNOWED IN

BELONGING

CHRISTMAS FOR COMMITMENTPHOBES

SMART GIRLS SERIES -All can be read as standalone stories

GIRL ON THE RUN – nominated for Joan Hessayon award

GIRL HAVING A BALL - nominated for Romantic Comedy of the Year 2017 RoNA awards

GIRL IN TROUBLE

GIRL AT CHRISTMAS - novella

Short Stories

KISSCHASE - A collection of six short stories

THE TRUTH ABOUT THE OTHER GUY

ONE NIGHT IN SHINING ARMOUR

Books Written as Jeevani Charika

CHRISTMAS AT THE PALACE – shortlisted for the Emma prize and The Pink Heart Soc reader choice

THIS STOLEN LIFE – Longlisted for Guardian Not The Booker Prize

A CONVENIENT MARRIAGE – shortlisted for RoNA contemporary romantic novel award 2020

Dedication

To my family. Always.

Acknowledgements

I never know where to start with these. Thank you to Ruth Long and Jen Hicks for their editing for this novella. Your feedback made this a much better story (and your enthusiasm for the story made me feel much better about it too!). I'm publishing this book while we're all in lockdown due to the Corona virus outbreak, but this book has no virus related shenanigans at all. Think of it as an alternative universe where the virus outbreak never happened and Cath Kidston never went bust.

There is a bit about Brexit though, because it was on my mind so much while I was writing it that I couldn't help it seeping into the story. Sorry about that.

Thanks to Fiona Goodman for listening to me wittering on about imaginary people during our post gym coffee. Thank you to Phillipa C and Isabelle D for hunting down typing errors (and the bit where I forgot which side of the road they drive on in Europe!).

Thanks to Jane Lovering and Jenni Fletcher, my tea and cake buddies for chivvying me along when I was at the 'I hate this book' stage of writing. As always, huge thanks to Ruth, Kate, Alison, Janet, Immi, and Sheila for their unwavering support that gets me through my crises both in writing and in real life.

Most of all thanks to my family for putting up with me. And thank *you* for reading.

About the Author

Rhoda Baxter writes contemporary romances with heart and a touch of cynicism. She also writes as Jeevani Charika. Her books have been shortlisted for awards such as the RoNA Romantic Comedy of the Year (in 2017 and in 2020), Love Stories Award (in 2015) and the Joan Hessayon Award (2012).

Rhoda started off as a microbiologist and then drifted out of research and into technology transfer. When choosing a penname, she was hit by a fit of nostalgia and named herself after the bacterium she studied during her PhD.

She has lived in a variety of places including Sri Lanka, Yap (it's a real place), Halifax, Oxford and Didcot (also a real place). She now lives with her young family in East Yorkshire, where there are enough tea shops to keep her happy.

You can find her wittering on about cake and science and other random things on her website (http://www.rhodabaxter.com), on Facebook[1], or on Twitter (@rhodabaxter). Please do say hello if you're passing.

You can also follow her on Bookbub[2].

Don't forget, you can get a free copy of one of her books by joining her reader newsletter[3].

---

1. https://en-gb.facebook.com/RhodaBaxterAuthor/

2. https://www.bookbub.com/authors/rhoda-baxter

3. https://www.subscribepage.com/CforC